To my alter ego!

Tony Holland

With the best wishes of the author

(signature)

THE WAR OF
CAMP OMONGO

The WAR of

RANDOM HOUSE · NEW YORK

CAMP
OMONGO

by *Burt Blechman*

Author of *HOW MUCH?*

to

J. T. MARSH

without whom the war
would not have taken place

THE WAR OF
CAMP OMONGO

AT BAY

WHEN THE TIDE WENT OUT, the bay's black bottom would spring to life. The bay would become a battlefield; muck and slime would become a seething mass of fighting, bleeding, battering warriors; and the hollow which had been filled with life would fill with death, as microscopic victors themselves became trapped in the drying mud, while the sun's flames grew hotter and the life-bearing tides retreated, until finally the whole shoreline smelled of it: of those who had lost—the dead, the decayed—and of those who had won and had eaten.

[3]

Man's smell, too, washed ashore by the tides, left to rot and putrefy in the sun's white heat: feces from Rome and Shanghai; an evacuation from the bowels of Louis XIV; stools from the Mussolinis; turds from popes and politicians, from businessmen, prostitutes, lawyers and landlords, from cops and killers, speculators and stick-up men, from generals and gangsters, psychologists and pimps—piling against the soft shore, no longer land or water but a mixture, as if the Biblical separation had never been completed here in an unnamed bay along the deserted shoreline of the East Bronx.

It was not the morning after Creation; it was not a week after, or a month after: you could tell that from the smell. It had taken millions of years of fighting and conquering to create what life had created, this corpse-strewn, stench-filled, fossil-lined shore.

Farther up, beyond the tide's reach, death too. Junk-pile pieces of rusted armor, broken gears, shells and grenades, axles and pinions. An old man poked through the rubble, searching for bits to scrape and polish, to sell again as new. An old man, dressed in fragments himself, wearing pieces of uniforms from obsolete countries, a torn sailor's cap, a bombardier's hole-pocked shoes, a marine's blood-stained jacket, a naval hero's corroded ceremonial gun belt. His house was made of scraps salvaged from the tides—cracked bricks, worn linoleum, splintered telephone poles, the splendiferous leftovers of some Golden Age, washed ashore, regurgitated, replaced.

The lopsided hovel at the edge of the muck marked the city's beginning. Farther back, the land became firmer, the stench less repugnant. Buildings grew higher and closer together; the soft dirt road became gravel, then cobblestones and finally asphalt.

Leaf-green awnings appeared, like a dense jungle sprung from the desert. First with numbers, then titles: one lived at the Tudor Arms, the George Washington, the Belle Vista.

Or one lived at the Versailles, in a narrow suite on the fifth floor, in an apartment piled high with treasures: a pair of Early American chests with reproduction knotholes; a set of Limoges cups and saucers, hand-painted in Tokyo; a worn Persian prayer rug made in Berlin, Maine; a medieval tapestry from Peru, Indiana; a Van Gogh sunflower printed on imitation canvas.

The apartment filled with the muffled roar of a waterfall in a mysterious, half-hidden grotto. The plastic seat slammed. Jacob's feces raced toward the bay.

The tide was coming in. Soon neighborhood kids would laugh and swim, and fat Italians on a day off would strain at the oars of rented boats. Randy liked it, even though his mother always told him it was full of dirt and disease, that he might catch something and give it to them at home, because only dirty Wops went there. He liked walking through the shallow water, the ooze squeezing between his toes. It was Easter Sunday. Randy wondered whether it had been lonely and still like this when that man sneaked out of his coffin: "Christ," he said it aloud, "Jesus Christ." His mother had warned him never to say that terrible name because it was a sin for a Jew even to think it, and anyhow where did he learn such things.

He saw himself in the shallow water. But it wasn't him, it was like a statue, the Statue of Liberty . . .

"A gift from France," boomed the loudspeaker, as the ferry neared the giant statue. The tourists were amazed.

"You don't get something for nothing," insisted his father. "Must have cost this country plenty."

The giantess towered above them threateningly. "That's what we fought for," continued his father, proudly. "Liberty. Freedom. Equality."

A sign, warning: jail for defacing the walls. He wondered where the jail was, but his father told him to keep still, it wasn't right to talk about that in the Statue of

Liberty . . . Freedom . . . Equality. They pushed ahead of the others.

From the boat, the face had been gentle and kind. But up close the stone eyes gazed bitterly, the fat lips curled in anger, the scarred skin blistered with pimples and sores.

Randy remembered what his father told him about America, the country where you could make something of yourself, become a success. Only in America could an immigrant—of course they were Americans now and proud of it—only here would Randy get ahead.

He walked past the junkman digging through the rubbish. Had he really been a farmer, planting things on this very spot? It sounded crazy. Randy's long shadow stretched almost to the tumble-down shack, bobbing up and down, twenty feet tall, like a circus freak. Everyone stared up, wondering what size shoe he wore and how much he ate for breakfast. "See my Giant Ring," he barked. "Only fifty cents. Amaze your friends." A little boy cried for one, but his mother said no. Randy, the giant, wanted to bend down and give it to him for free, but the boss was watching.

He walked into the Versailles lobby. He felt small again.

The elevator creaked toward the fifth floor. Randy looked at the writing, some of it in chalk, some in lipstick, some carved. With his mother and father, he tried not to notice, but alone, he liked it—it got him excited, made him hot. FUCK YOU, carved in the plywood door. MIKE EATS CUNT. FATSO TAKES IT UP THE ASS. And the obliterations, PUCK and POOR. The janitor tried to fill it in and scrub it off, but next day it would always be there again. "Hoodlums," he'd insist. "Can't be no one in this house." The question: IS DOLLY A GOOD LAY???; and its answer: I'LL SAY!!! The command SUCK, the hot aspiration MEET ME HERE AT 10 FOR A BLOW JOB, and the sweet lullaby composed by Bertha Goldstein, whose mother had warned her about boys, FUCK ME BABY I LUV IT, signed with her pen name, GUESS WHO.

[6]

"It's about time," his father roared.

"Jacob, please," said his mother. "A little dignity."

"What's the trouble?" asked Randy.

"Something wonderful," said his mother. "CAMP OMONGO! You won. The scholarship."

"Can't they give it to somebody else?"

His mother drew back as if she'd been embracing a pig. "What do you mean, darling?" She looked like a little girl with innocent eyelashes.

"I just mean I'd rather stay home. I didn't like that guy Steiner."

"Guy!" yelled Mr. Levine. "Where'd you pick up an expression like that, in the elevator?"

"Jacob, leave this to me," said his mother. "Randy darling. It's a swell camp, a camp where you'll meet nice young Jewish boys. Boys who'll be marvelous contacts later in life. Why do you think your father never got ahead?" Mr. Levine looked away. "No contacts! He wasn't lucky enough to have considerate parents. But you, you're so lucky you should be crying for happiness." She raced to the bureau for a handkerchief. "I'm so happy I can't help it." She kissed Randy wetly on the forehead.

Randy was ashamed. Every time she cried, and he'd seen her do it whenever she wanted something, he knew it was his fault. "All right," he muttered. "Yeah. I'm going."

She put her arms around him, rubbing her soft black hair against his face. The way she'd hugged him the time he got lost coming home from the dentist. The way she hugged him in the dentist's chair. It wouldn't hurt, and there'd be a lollipop if he was good, and he shouldn't look at the giant pincers. She held his hand, smiling, gently squeezing. Suddenly her grip tightened. She was holding him against the chair, holding him down, his own mother! The dentist's face drew closer, tiny beads of sweat on his forehead and black pores on his nose. Did he need a shot?—How

[7]

much?—Five. Her grip tightened. Randy was a brave boy and could stand the pain. The giant pliers forced into his mouth, searching, yanking. Then they were in the subway, he was leaning against her warm, woolly coat. Hurry! She was gone, no, she was inside the train, her face pressed to the glass, trying to tell him something he couldn't hear, her mouth opening and closing, faster and faster. He started to cry. The dentist had forgotten the lollipop. She'd be mad. He shouldn't have let go of her. But she put her arms around him. He was sorry, he'd never do it again and he loved her, he loved her. He'd never leave her, never.

The train inside him roared, dragging him away, but he tried to hold on to her. He'd never leave, he'd never go to that damned camp, never. That was all there was to it.

"Mama, Mama, stop crying," shouted his father. "You win, didn't you hear? He said he's going already."

She lifted her handkerchief and smiled.

EMBARKATION

$1.40. JACOB LEVINE GROANED. Why couldn't they take the subway? Always trying to be fancy. Who'd see them, anyhow?

$1.45. And that excuse about the heavy trunk. God damn it, for this price, he'd carry it on his back!

$1.50. At least they could have caught the train uptown, and save on the fare. No, not Madam Esther Levine the Third, Grand Central Station or nothing.

$1.60. The impression, that's all she cared about, holding hands with her little scholarship kid in this high-class taxi, while the rich campers were sweating it out in the subway.

$1.75! That machine was fixed! Jacob groaned again, rapidly multiplying quarter-miles times the rate, plus ten per cent for error.

Mrs. Levine glared a stern warning: stop, immediate, or there'll be trouble.

"Two dollars!" cried Mr. Levine.

"All right, Jacob. We can read, too."

"I wish I'd bought the gray suit," said Randy.

"That lemon!" sneered his mother. "The salesman was laughing up his sleeve because he couldn't wait to get rid of it."

"I only hope Oronsky doesn't say anything about my taking the day off," muttered his father.

"All of Ohrbach's was watching," continued his mother. "You're lucky I was there to pick the herringbone."

"Best herringbone-picker in the business," cracked his father.

"Not in front of the boy!" She tried to smile.

The meter ticked away. Mr. Levine pretended it was the tick-tick-tick of his assembly-line sewing machine. It was comforting.

"Beautiful!" exclaimed Mrs. Levine, looking down from the balcony onto the huge main floor filled with thousands of screaming children and hysterical parents. "Like one big happy family. Come, let's join."

Behind the flags and placards loomed an immense missile, like the cross of some crusading army of children, painted in bright kindergarten reds and blues. "There's my boss," said Mr. Levine, pointing toward a group under the banner: CAMP OMONGO.

"Mr. Oronsky, my husband and I want to thank you for what you've done for our son," said Mrs. Levine.

[9]

"Lousy," he shouted. "Business is just plain old lousy."

Randy tugged at his mother's dress and whispered past the dangling rhinestone earring, "Do I still . . . do I still have to go?" She looked faint, as if she'd been threatened with rape.

"Tent Thirty-eight," she screamed. "Allow me," she turned to the counselor, "to introduce. Me, I'm Mrs. Levine. And there's my husband." Mr. Levine stumbled forward.

She smiled brightly at Randy and handed him a dollar, making sure the counselor noticed. "Buy yourself something to read," she laughed. "Keep the change."

Randy walked to the missile. "How far can that thing go?" he asked the guard.

"Military secret," snapped the soldier, as if addressing a spy.

They all had secrets, he thought, and nobody made them tell. But Randy always gave in. The way he did with the animals. They were dirty and diseased, for farmers, not for nice, clean Jewish boys, his mother always said. He kept the turtle in a secret box, and stole bread to feed it. He took it for swims in the bathtub behind the locked door. He saved his allowance for a glass tank and three goldfish. Then he hid them on a shelf at the very top of the closet where his mother never cleaned. He'd put the tank on a table and watch it for hours, the fish swimming under the toy bridge, and the turtle, the sleepy-head turtle snoring away on his rock. One day he bought a deep-sea diver and a painted castle and bright shiny pebbles to cover the bottom. One of the goldfish came to live in the castle, and the other two goldfish chased each other around and around, and the turtle just went on sleeping. Then he would hear his parents outside, telling him to open up, not to lock his door like a common thief. Randy would say no and his mother would change her tone. What was so secret he had to shut the door in their faces? He'd hide the tank in the closet and open.

They'd storm in, his mother stomping and shouting, maybe even giving him a slap, not too hard, just enough to hurt. There were no secrets in the Levine family. If only he would tell her, his own mother, please, tell, tell. Then she'd look through his drawers and behind his books and in his toy chest, everywhere. But she never even came close. He was a thief, a common thief, and if he loved her he wouldn't try to keep secrets. She kissed him all over and she begged him, if he loved her, if he loved her even a little, to tell her, please. He felt sick, because he'd made her cry and it was wrong to hide things like a dirty sneak. Finally he told. She gave him a quick kiss. She ran for the ladder and dragged down the tank. Crazy, keeping those carriers of disease, that's all they were. He begged her not to hurt them, they were his friends. She told him not to say that when the only real friends he had were his mother and father, and that he must get rid of this filth. Immediate. His health came first and foremost, and she dumped the water and the fish and the turtle into the toilet. She took the castle and the deep-sea diver and smashed them into a million pieces. He cried. He wanted to take the fish and turtle to the bay and free them. With one quick snap she flushed them down. He covered his ears. He could hear them screaming in the pipes. Screaming. He wanted to kill her, to grab her neck and hold her in the toilet until she couldn't breathe, push her all the way in, and pull the handle and flush her down the drain. He was crying because he hated her. He'd never tell another secret as long as he lived.

"Mr. Steiner!" She was talking to the camp director. Steiner looked puzzled. "My son, Randy. He's so happy about the scholarship I can't tell you. Randy, tell him."

"Yeah," Randy shifted his weight. "I'm happy."

Steiner checked his watch. He blew his whistle. The campers began to line up, like well-trained insects. Steiner smiled. The school year was over. At last. Ten months in a classroom filled with babbling idiots, ten months teaching algebra and geometry to kids who could hardly spell, hardly add, with minds like strainers, catching only dirt, smut, sex. At Omongo it was different. At least it would be, if he could get the camp on its feet again. Quit teaching. Omongo was his life. He'd built it out of a forsaken strip of woods in the Adirondack wilderness. Like a God he'd turned it into a garden. He'd rather see Omongo crumble into bankruptcy than surrender to that loud-mouthed Oronsky bastard.

Steiner frowned. A six-year-old was refusing to get into line. No, he kept shouting, I'm not going! His mother shrugged. He had to, they were going on a trip, there was no more room at home, there was no more home, it was all locked up.

Uncle Bob Cohen, his counselor, shoved the little troublemaker into the line of Midgets where he belonged. The boy screamed and kicked. Uncle Bob squeezed tighter, until the crying was nothing but a ripple of muffled sobs, and Cohen was grinning.

Randy went with the thirteen-year-olds. Mrs. Levine was still questioning their counselor. "You come from a lovely part, Mr. Tannenbaum. Personally I've never visited Mamaroneck, but in the papers you should notice the high rentals they're charging out there."

Steiner blew another whistle. The Midget was still struggling. Uncle Bob got a half nelson around his tiny neck. Mrs. Levine looked for her hankie. What lovely children, she thought, so well behaved.

They started marching. There was too much noise and shouting for Randy to hear his mother yell to brush his teeth, to wash before eating, to wash after he went. It was like a Victory Parade down Broadway, with two hundred jubilant campers marching home from war, their parents screaming at the top of their lungs, throwing ticker tape and confetti, cheering from the sidewalks, welcoming them home. Only they weren't coming home; they were leaving. For good, weeks and weeks. And the shouting, hand-waving parents weren't greeting them, they were saying good-bye, and the good-bye meant: no, don't leave us, please. Mrs. Levine turned away, quickly, before little Randy could see her crying, crying because she wanted him to grow up, to become something, to succeed.

The campers broke free, into a frenzied, howling mob, racing toward the coffin-like cars, piling through the narrow doors, fighting for the best seats. Midgets got pushed into the aisles to make room for Juniors, Juniors were jerked out to give way to Intermediates, Intermediates were thrown out by Seniors to make room for themselves. The parents were gone; it was everyone for himself.

A gang attacked an empty seat, splitting it open with a pocket knife, and throwing the stuffing in the air, drowning the car in white bitter snow. A conductor rushed in. Someone stuck out his foot; the conductor fell. His watch shattered on the floor, a thousand gold and silver pieces, a shiny spring bobbing up and down like the beating of a dying heart. Someone grabbed it for a souvenir. The air filled with projectiles: tennis balls, sandwiches, comic books.

Suddenly Randy saw her. Outside. His mother. Looking for him. He rushed to the window. Mama! Mama!

She was crying. Her face was old and wrinkled. She stumbled forward, as if to chase him, smiling like a painted statue. The train began to move like a funeral procession. Faster, faster, past the brightly lit platform, into the deep black tunnel. He pressed his face to the glass. She was behind him. He felt himself sinking. It was too late and she was far, far behind. Someone grabbed his ankles and he went down; he was crawling, punching, kicking, scratching like the others, and she was gone, she was gone.

[13]

REVEILLE

||||||||||||||||||||||||||||||||||||||||||||||||||

A BLACK LIMOUSINE zoomed between the tents. A sleepy-
looking kid with dark hair and a face pale as a baseball
climbed out. He flopped on the nearest bed.

He pulled a couple of aspirins from his shirt pocket
and swallowed them. What a farewell party! There must
have been thirty guys at least. With his mom in Miami and
his pop in Mexico someplace trying to get that divorce, he
had the whole duplex to himself. He called up the gang,
even guys he didn't know. The chauffeur had to put on
his butler's uniform and serve drinks, and the maid dished
out all that fancy food. O'Donnell was drunk right from the
start, and the downstairs neighbor called up because the
music was too wild. Go to hell, he told him. The chauffeur
tried to quiet them down and he said shut up because that's
what he got paid for. The music was getting hotter and
hotter. The people downstairs called again. Madam was not
at home, he told them, imitating the maid, and go blow it
out their asshole. Scaretto was puking. O'Donnell was out
cold. Norman turned the record player louder. Bull's-eye,
he shouted, let's have a game. He got up on the coffee
table. That big painting of his mom. Whango! The bottom
of her dress was covered with anchovies. Calazzo splashed
her in the puss. The gin dripped down her neck. A beer
bottle, bamo! Right through her smile. He'd never had so
much fun in his life. Everyone was drinking and laughing

and jumping around. He grabbed the long kitchen knife and took another swallow. His ears were ringing. He drew back his arm. His hands shook with excitement. He flung the silver knife through the air with a loud swish! going straight for her, WHAM—right through her canvas heart. He fell to the floor and they were all yelling what a terrific shot. Everyone started throwing things again and he wanted to stop them but he didn't, he didn't, he lay there, yelling hit her, again, harder, again, and he was crawling all over her precious velvet carpet on his hands and knees like a dirty little cockroach, yelling hit her, hit her!

The chauffeur lugged the trunk into Tent 38. "Get your ass over to the flag-raising," snapped a counselor, pulling Norman toward the Parade Grounds.

Two hundred campers, their faces like masks, gazed up at the flagpole. The tallest tree in the whole forest had been stripped of its thick bark and its green leaves, had been filed and planed, sanded and shellacked. On the very top Steiner had nailed an eagle bought at some auction. Below the eagle, now flaked and rotten, hung the American flag, and below that, the red and blue banner of Omongo. High and solitary, the flagpole was planted firmly on the flat, grassless plain, as if the shell of a Gothic church had suddenly collapsed—the sculptured naves, the gilded angels, the innocent saints—leaving only the wooden spire and its two gaudy banners, a symbol of faith, pointing upward at an empty sky toward something which, like the tree itself, no longer existed.

Two hundred voices echoed across the lake: the booming basses of the counselors, the determined baritones of the Seniors, the blurred falsettos and wavering low notes of the Intermediates, the shrill tenors of the Juniors, and the pure birdlike sopranos of the Midgets. Fusing together, the voices bound in a spell, some hypnotic trance, a mystic union. ". . . the Republic for which it stands . . ." they affirmed

[15]

grimly, as if the flag was being surrounded, threatened, about to be attacked. ". . . under God, Indivisible . . ." they chanted as if at a synagogue, trying to sound as if they understood the mysterious words. ". . . liberty and justice for all."

Rabbi Yeslin stepped in front of the flagpole. Steiner had warned him to keep it short. He began to pray in a low, droning monotone, his earnest face gazing one way, then another. He turned his palms upward to implore, down to deplore. His eyes searched the dawn-red sky as he spoke of God, examined the gravel as he spoke of evil.

He gazed at the heavens. They waited impatiently for the benediction. He swatted a mosquito. He continued, speaking of mercy . . . mercy, his arms forming a chalice, as if to catch the mercy as it fell like rain water from the heavens. His hands gyrated upward. *Now,* they prayed, *finish now.* His palms revolved again, slyly, in little sneaky movements, pulling away from the sky, turning mournfully toward the ground. "Pray with me," he intoned. And they prayed. *Now.* "God." *Now.* "Almighty, who has created this lovely camp . . ."

What the hell! Who else but he, Steiner, had created it? Out of nothing, a wilderness. His wrinkles deepened. What was the new rabbi preaching about?

Steiner strode to the microphone. "Fellow tribesmen," he announced, drowning out Rabbi Yeslin's hurried *Amen.* "To those from seasons past, and to those new to our reservation and its proud heritage—welcome!

"Twenty-three years ago today, the first Omongos began their climb toward that pinnacle we call success. Here they were trained: trained to think, trained to obey, trained to defend the American Way. Here they developed that fighting spirit which has made America great, and which has made Omongo great. One of those boys is now a prominent manufacturer of bomb shelters. One is a famous adver-

tising executive. Another, this country's greatest comedian
—you all know his name: Eddie Hackstein!"

A chorus of oh's and ah's from the ranks. Steiner smiled
knowingly. His hands gripped the mike. "Fellow tribesmen,
you may ask what is Omongo. Who were those forgotten
people, where did they live? I will tell you," he whispered,
about to reveal the secret. "The Omongos lived right here,
in these very forests, along the shores of this very lake.
Other tribes retreated in cowardice; other tribes retreated in
defeat. But the Omongos, the fiercest and most savage of
all the woodland tribes, refused to join. They were determined to win a total victory or a total defeat. They knew
that victory is either complete or it isn't victory at all."

Steiner lowered his voice, reverently. "Fellow tribesmen,
we all know what happened: the Omongos went down to
defeat. They preferred death to living in default, death to
living in disgrace, death to living in dishonor." His voice rose
triumphantly. "That, fellow tribesmen, is our proud heritage. Like the Omongos, we must fight without ever giving
quarter, without ever backing down, without ever succumb-
ing to a peace filled with the filthy poison of contentment,
with a willingness to be second, and if second, why not
third, and if third, why not last?

"No!" he shrieked. "It is our duty as Omongos and as
loyal Americans to be winners. If a manufacturer, a winning
manufacturer, miles ahead of your competitors. If in law,
be a lawyer who can win over any jury. As a doctor, win
a large and respected practice."

Steiner snapped to attention. "Fellow tribesmen, we
belong to a winning country. Who won the French and
Indian War, the War of 1812, the Mexican War, the Civil
War, the Spanish-American War? Who won the First
World War, the Second World War and all the other wars?
America! America never has, and never shall lose a war be-

cause we would rather disappear from the face of this earth, yes, and take the earth with us, than be defeated."

The campers wanted to cheer. Steiner held up his arms and continued. "Now we all know that the first Omongos did not have the physical might. But today we have tremendous resources. All we need is that glorious will-to-win. And my friends, if the day should ever come when we accept defeat or compromise, then our courageous history, our splendid Camp Omongo, will come to an end." They could feel the lump in his throat. Then it began to rise, the lump, the voice, higher, passionate, filling the woods and the sky.

"That is why we need, why America needs Omongo. To train boys to fight for the love of fighting, to win for the love of winning. On the baseball field, we will bat our way to victory. At the rifle range, we will shoot our way to victory! Because that's what our country is—a victorious nation, a nation of men imbued with the will-to-win, in sports, in business, in war. Every one of you here has an opportunity. Take it. Use it. Learn to compete, to excel, to become worth-while citizens of our brave land."

Steiner pointed at the rotting eagle. "Over us today, high above us, flies the flag of the United States of America, and under it the splendid flag of Omongo. I want to say to you now, that before long I will place before you two flagpoles. One for the great emblem of the United States. The other for our own proud banner. One next to the other, side by side, flying together in the same clear breeze, together under the same bright sky, together above the same hallowed ground. Because, fellow tribesmen, they belong together, because they are one and inseparable, because they are triumphant and everlasting. Because—fellow tribesmen—America and Omongo are one and the same!"

OFF TO A GOOD START

"JACKY APPLEBAUM," said the waiter, brushing the hair out of his eyes. "Working my way through college, and every little bit helps."

"Don't expect anything from that guy," warned Mike, pointing at Randy. "He's on a scholarship. Not paying a red cent. You'll be lucky if his old man's check don't bounce."

"Hey, how come there's only four of you? Don't tell me I got short-changed!" growled the waiter.

"He just got here," said Mel.

"In a private car," said Randy. "With a chauffeur."

"You ought to get a nice big tip from him," said Mel.

"That's if you treat us right," said Mike. "We'll put in a good word for you."

Smiling Steiner pulled out the chair like a servant in a high-class hotel. "Sit yourself right down, son," he told Norman. "Boys, Norm's new at Omongo. I want him to feel at home right off the bat. Sid," he turned to the counselor, "take good care of our boy."

Jacky Applebaum grinned. His teeth were yellow. Norman got the first bowl of oatmeal; Randy, the last.

"This your first year, too?" asked Sid.

"Are you kidding! I been here four years in a row," said Mel, proudly, "and my pal Mike's been here five."

"I guess you must like it pretty well, then."

Mike wiped the oatmeal from his mouth with the back of his wrist. "Up here you know where you stand. It's not like at school where only the grinds count."

"You're right," said Randy. "In the school I go to, even the guys on teams have to be bookworms."

Mike tapped his fork against the table. "Who are you kidding, Levine? You're probably the biggest grind there is."

Randy shook his head guiltily.

"Well, if you're not, your old man sure is. Put him on piece work, my dad says, and he'll bust his balls just to make ten cents an hour more."

"Relax," urged Sid, trying not to sound embarrassed.

Mike poked his friend. "You know Levine here lives in the cheapest part of the Bronx?"

"Money isn't everything," said Sid, thinking of his parents' two tiny rooms in Mamaroneck. "What difference does it make?"

"A lot," said Mel.

"This camp ain't a poorhouse," snapped Mike.

"Can the crap," said the new kid, Norman.

Mike smiled. "If you like hanging around with people on relief, Greenberg, you're going to be out of place here. Unless you want to be friends with this jerk."

"Since you like money so much," said Norman, "let me tell you—my family's got enough dough to make yours look like peanuts. Next to mine, your old man's a cheap, lousy piker!"

Mike sprang up, Sid looked worried, Mel drew back, Randy turned away, Steiner blew his whistle. Breakfast was over.

They raced between the tents, old shacks with torn-up screens and creaky stairs. Jerky little bungalows! Randy was tired from the long train ride. But there was no time to rest. Always telling you do this, do that. Like school, only worse. At least everyone *knew* school was bad. But here it was supposed to be fun. Some vacation!

Tent 38. They were already inside, bellowing, their fists raised. It was 38 all right, like the number of a prison cell.

"Get your things off my bed," yelled Mel. "It was mine last year, and it's mine this year, too. Anyway, I always sleep next to Mike."

"Nothing doing," said Norman.

Mel decided to work on that other dope, Randy. "Move your junk, kid," he said, dragging his trunk toward Randy's bed.

"I wouldn't if I were you," warned Greenberg.

"What's the difference?" asked Randy.

"You move just because this guy tells you to," said Norm, "before you know it, you'll be nothing but his stooge."

Randy nodded, but it didn't mean yes, it just meant he didn't know.

"Levine," commanded Mike, putting on his sweatshirt, "are you moving your stuff or do I have to move it for you?"

"What the heck," said Randy, his voice cracking, "what do I care. I'll take the other bed." Greenberg stared at him as if he were a freak.

"Hey, fellas," shouted Sid, enthusiastically, "take your things and get over to the Parade Grounds."

"Hey, fellas," shouted Mel, imitating the new counselor, "don't forget your baseball mitts."

"And say, fellas," said Mike, lunging at Mel, "don't forget your balls."

Fat Stuff Halpern took command. Norm Greenberg, the shortest, was first, then Randy Levine, Mel Kahn, and Mike Oronsky, the biggest. The fat kid led them down the dusty road.

"Hey, Fat Stuff," shouted Mike. "Where'd you get a name like that?"

"Three guesses," cried Mel.

"Breakfast, lunch and dinner!"

"Wise guys," grinned Fat Stuff, his mouthful of braces sparkling in the sun.

"Gimme a cigarette," said Mike, grabbing Mel's pack and dumping it into his pocket. Mel smiled, as if he were used to it.

"Cut the smoking," yelled Fat Stuff.

"Up yours," said Mel, grabbing.

"Cut it out," pleaded Fat Stuff, his hands a pair of fig leaves.

"He's only acting," said Mike. "He really likes to be goosed, don't you, Fat Stuff?"

"With that new secret weapon of his, it's no joke," said Mel. "A super rear-end bumper."

"C'mon, you guys," said Mike, "let's gang up on him."

Randy made a sheepish move. "Watch out!" called Mel, and before Randy knew what was happening, Halpern's fat fingers were groping him.

"Goose him back," said Mike.

"Watch it," warned Mel, "there's Gans."

Bud Gans, president of the Junior class, head of Interfraternity Council, captain of the baseball team, champion of the fencing conference, listed in Who's Who in American Colleges as a star and in the registrar's files as a C minus, looked them in the eye. Everyone became serious, almost glum: it was the beginning of a new season.

"Toss the bat!" A chorus of held breaths, of whispered benedictions. Hand over hand, like a pair of snakes, they crawled up the shaft to the knob. The winner smiled. He had first choice.

Enemies on the same team stood awkwardly, then, without saying a word, shook hands. Friends found themselves no longer buddies, but Sioux or Iroquois, split apart by a single word, staring at each other, enemies. The anxious leftovers turned their heads from side to side. Would they be picked so late everyone would know they were no good, that they were scraping the bottom of the barrel?

The captains scowled, as if inspecting a bunch of sloppy recruits. "Hey, Greenberg," pointing to that rotten apple, Norman. "How good are you?"

"That's for you to find out."

"Wise-guy," said the Sioux captain. "All right, you're on."

Randy looked down at his feet. A grasshopper. It looked dead, afraid to move. That's how he felt.

"You any good?" demanded the captain of the Iroquois.

Randy's voice squeaked. "I've only played a couple of times. Maybe you better take that other guy."

"Shit," muttered Mike, "I guess we get you whether we want you or not, Levine."

"How's it feel to be last?" said Mel. Randy tried to smile. "Get this guy, he thinks it's a big joke."

"Cut the kidding," said Mike, "or we'll shove that smile right down your lousy throat. We're out to win here. This ain't no comic-strip camp."

Randy pounded his glove. A brand-new one, the first he'd ever owned, approved by Stan Mjukislyzk, champion fielder. Even had his signature to prove it. Left field, the daisies they called it. Mel hurled a practice ball.

"Thata baby, thata baby, that's puttin' it right where it belongs," yelled the pitcher.

"Talk it up, talk it up out there," shouted Mike.

"C'mon," muttered Randy, feeling dopey, "throw it."

The ball! Coming straight toward him. "Back up," they shouted. He couldn't move; he couldn't think. He just stood, watching the tiny speck falling, getting closer. He stuck out his mitt: Stan Mjukislyzk, the magic glove, catch it, please!

[23]

They were yelling at him, swearing. He raced after the ball. "What the hell d'you call that?" cried the second baseman.

"I'll do better next time," Randy whispered. He wanted to run into the woods, to hide where they couldn't find him, behind the rocks, the bushes, to hide from the burning hot field with its screaming voices and slashing bats and threats and groans and curses.

BY THE STILL WATERS

THE WATER WAS ALWAYS CHILLY early in the season. Cohen liked it this way, better than at the end of the summer when the lake would be like the steam-heated pool of a Catskill resort, where dying old people, half-asleep, coiled in reclining chairs to watch swimmers, not really swimmers at all but floaters, inflated corpses, drifting on the surface of life. Cohen liked it cold, alive, the beginning of a new year.

He checked the rope. It was last season's, frayed and rotting. It would have to do. He looked at the campers coming toward the pier, their pale torsos bouncing up and down as they passed the neat racks of red and blue canoes, shouting, joking, disorganized. How could you teach them to swim when they weren't interested in anything but their little games, their little tricks, their little bodies? He wheeled around. The towel snapping, the laughing died down.

"Most of you know the score. The rules are simple. Don't swim farther than you're able to, and don't show off.

When I blow my whistle, obey. Be a wise-guy and you'll get straightened out."

Randy tightened his drawstrings. This was different from baseball. He was good at swimming. "You like this?" he asked Norman.

"How the hell should I know," said Norman, "never did it before."

"Never went swimming! I thought everybody knew how."

"Now you know better."

"At the end of the year," said the swimming counselor, "every guy who wins the Shark emblem, I mean if any of you do"—they were smiling, confident, the emblems sewn firmly on their trunks—"gets a chance at a special medal, a big gold one."

Cohen looked stern. "All you guys that don't know how to swim yet, step out. We may as well start at the beginning."

Norman moved forward. The others grinned. Maybe they were bluffing. You had to bluff around here. "Sissy," someone yelled. "Get him a pair of Cadillac water wings, with a chauffeur to tow it."

"I'm not going in," said Norman.

Cohen's arms reached out of the water like fangs. "I'm gonna teach you how to swim," he threatened, "if it's the last thing I do. Now kick them goddam legs."

"F' Christ's sake, hold on," shouted Norman. "You're drowning me."

"Oh save me, save me, Daddy! I'm sinking," yelled Mike.

Norman scrambled up the ladder. The campers gathered around him like vultures, laughing and jeering. "You can take your lousy swimming and shove it," cried Norman, racing away toward the tents.

"Poor sport," yelled Cohen.

[25]

Norman sat down on his bunk. He peeled off the clammy bathing suit, pulling down the wet jock. He lay naked on his bright blue Omongo blanket, looking at the unpainted rafters, at a spider way up in the corner, in his trap, waiting. How'd he ever get roped into this? It was all right for her to send him off here, while she tramped around the country from one hotel to another, "visiting." That's why she got rid of him, so she could do whatever she wanted. That's why she sent him to this concentration camp, this high-class reformatory. That's all it was, the lousy trees, like prison bars, and for guards those big-ox counselors. That Cohen bastard almost drowned him. If only his own gang were here! Just for an hour, even a few minutes. They'd rough him up so he'd never forget.

Like the time they got that flower peddler, a wrinkled-up old man everyone hated. Maybe it was the way he was always so extra polite, bowing and scraping in his suit and black bow tie. Once he even gave Norman a flower for free. Norman threw it in the trash barrel. One night the gang cornered the dope and shoved him into the gutter, his suit and face splattered with mud. He didn't yell or say anything, just lay there on his back, like a stiff with his funeral flowers. They scooped up the blossoms and threw them around like colored snowballs, red, green, pink. The old man still wasn't doing anything, like he really was dead. That got them scared. "Let's get out of here," shouted Norman. Scaretto looked at the old man's face, and suddenly, for no reason at all, he kicked him, hard, in the ribs. Norman could hear them snapping against Scaretto's shoe.

The spider fell. The bugle cried. Like someone far away calling for help. He lay on his sack, his naked body stiff and sweating, the old man's cries ringing in his ears.

CONVOCATION

THE JAP HOLLERED bloody murder; the American, smiling with enthusiasm, thrust his clean bayonet, then jerked it out again; the corpse sprawled at his feet, a well-done shish-kebab. The American sharpened his knife, his fork . . .

"Watch out!" cried Mike.

"Behind you!" said Mel.

The Marine turned. Another Jap, smiling, pointed his rifle. The American, smiling back, greeted him with a loud hello of bullets. The sly Jap tumbled to the ground, the slanted eyes frozen to his face.

"Maybe he's fooling," whispered Fat Stuff, as if thirty bullets weren't enough. The Marine gazed down innocently. A sudden close-up. The Jap's forefinger, gnarled and dirty, squeezed the rusty trigger.

"Look out!" screamed Fat Stuff.

The American jumped, pulled out his gun and let him have it. Another thirty bullets. The Jap rolled over. This time the Marine was taking no chances. He slipped his bayonet deep into the enemy's ribs, twisted it as if carving a turkey. The blood spurted. The Jap quivered. The lights went on.

"Hey, Levine, how about giving me what you're eating and I'll give you a nickel," said Fat Stuff.

"I already ate half."

[27]

"O.K., so I'll buy the half you got left." Randy stopped eating. "A nickel," he repeated.

"For half? What's the trick?"

"What are you complaining about?" said Fat Stuff. "You're the one who's making the profit."

"Think they got a chance of breaking out?"

"Those Chinks?" said Fat Stuff. "They'll never be able to stand up to the Americans." He let the gooey chocolate melt in his mouth. "They'll butcher those Chinks alive."

"They're not Chinks," said Mel, "they're Japs."

"What's the difference," said Fat Stuff. "They're yellow, ain't they?"

The lights went out. The talking stopped. The American started wiping the stains off his bayonet.

"Behind you!" cried Mel.

Too late. The Jap came leaping down from the tree like an ape. The American reached for his knife; the Jap grabbed his arm. It was one of those tricky jiujitsu holds. The American let go. His knife flew into the bushes.

No! A shout rose from the darkened hall. He was going to fight it out with his bare fists, hand to hand. Cries of pain erupted from the blackness. The dirty Jap was working his jiujitsu trick again, tightening his grip.

"Hit him back!"

"Get him!"

The Marine tripped.

"No fair!" shouted Fat Stuff.

"Dirty!" cried Mel.

The American was stronger, a hundred times stronger. He kicked. The Jap fell in a heap, clutching his belly. In a flash the American was on top.

"Get him! Beat him!"

And the Marine pounded the living daylights out of the dirty Jap, pounded him with his bare fists, the old-fashioned way with a right to the jaw, a left, another right. The Jap lay there on the ground, looking at the enthusiastic knuckles.

"Get up," whispered Randy. He always felt sorry for the guy who was losing. Even if it was only a crummy Jap.

"Hit him!" they shouted. "Again, again!"

Randy felt like a spy, a sneak, as if all of them, the campers, the counselors, were yelling at *him*, cursing him, calling him a traitor.

The film broke. They groaned.

"It'll be a couple of minutes, boys," cried a nervous voice from the projection room.

"Take a breather," shouted a counselor.

"Why do they always stop just when it gets good?" asked Fat Stuff.

"Hey, Levine," said Mel, "who the hell you for, anyhow? I could swear you were cheering for them Japs."

"You're kidding?" Randy got up. "What do you think I am, a spy or something?" He headed for the john.

Randy looked in the mirror. A blackhead. With his fingers like a pair of pincers, he pinched it out. He felt as if he'd been cleansed of something deforming.

"They spread if you squeeze 'em."

It was Norman, wearing a filthy Omongo sweatshirt. "I'm sorry about what happened," said Randy. "I mean this afternoon."

"If you were really so sorry you could have done something."

"At least they didn't make you miss the movie. It's pretty terrific."

"The hell with the movie," said Norm. "They can take it and shove it. I'm not going to be a good little camper like you just to see one."

"You're sore because they wanted to confine you."

"I'm sore 'cause they tried to drown me. Cohen and those palsy-walsy friends of yours."

[29]

"I don't have any friends," said Randy. It sounded stupid. "I mean except maybe you."

The picture had already started. Randy slumped into his seat. There was just this one last Jap, way up on the very top of the mountain. The Americans went after him. They were hauling something, dragging it up the side of the mountain.

"Flame thrower!" cried Mel.

"That'll get him!" shouted Mike.

The Jap poked his head from behind the rock. It was a mistake. The Americans whipped out their big black machine. The Jap aimed his tinny little rifle. Too late.

The flames were all around him. First his jacket, then his shirt, then his undershirt, then his skin, bubbling and popping.

"Look at him sizzle!"

"French-fried Jap!"

"In on him, in on him!"

A squad of Americans ran up the ridge, indifferent to danger, ducking, rising again, pulling, from nowhere, an immense spick-and-span flag. The Stars and Stripes! The music swelled in a mighty refrain: *The Star-Spangled Banner*.

It made your hair stand on end, as the hymn roared from the speaker, as the camera flashed a close-up of the Jap's twisting lips, as the flames grew higher and higher, hotter and hotter.

"Get 'im!"

"Burn 'im!"

He wasn't burning. He was melting! Right in front of their eyes. The Americans smiled, with their flag soaring, with their flames glowing hotter, with their yells getting louder, and the hollering of that Jap, all mingling with the third stanza. It made you want to get up and cheer.

"Burn 'im!" they cried. "Burn 'im, burn 'im, burn 'im."

The Jap joined in with his crazy *oink-oink, oink-oink*.
Everyone was laughing, laughing so hard they could hardly
keep from crying. It was so funny, with that Jap and his
crazy words. *Oink-oink, oink-oink.* And that body of his,
sizzling like a hot dog.

Get up, get up, Randy kept whispering to the Jap.
Fat Stuff was screaming, laughing; Mike was laughing,
too, and so were Mel and Cohen and Gans and Steiner
and his two hundred jubilant campers; and the Jap with
his blood leaking out across the screen, drowning the hall
in his murderous, fearful yelps. The camp filled with it,
the laughs and the clapping and the *oink-oink* screams, echoing through the woods, past the canoes. The cries of laughter and the cries of pain grew louder, swelling, fusing, until
they were one—a joyful, excruciating roar. The music
stopped; the picture ended; the bright beam flickered out.
For a moment there was nothing but darkness and silence,
as if suddenly, here at Omongo, there were no longer any
people.

INSPECTION

"UP AND AT 'EM!" Cohen pounded on the door. "Inspection
this morning."

Mike shoved back his blankets, sat up, then slid to the
floor, his hand reaching automatically for his shorts. Five
seasons of Omongo had taught him to cut off his dreams
sharply, one snip of the scissors, and he was back in routine.

[31]

"Get a load of pretty-boy Greenberg," he said, shaking Norman's rickety bed frame. "Still thinks he's on Park Avenue."

"Leave me alone," muttered Norman, turning over sleepily.

"'Leave me alone,'" sneered Mike. "Little boy blue wants to blow his horn." He ripped off the blanket. The cold air hit Norm like a fist. "Gee, pretty boy sleeps raw."

"He's got a hard on," said Mel. "No wonder he didn't want to get up. Who'd you dream about, pretty boy?"

"Let's get going," cried Sid, blushing. "It's late."

Flinn and Cohen marched in. "Atten-shun!" barked Flinn, his cold eyes taking in every detail. Like rubber bands, they pulled themselves taut.

"You call those hospital corners?" accused Cohen.

"What's a hospital corner?" asked Randy, his voice shaking.

"Beds," shouted Flinn, pulling Randy's blankets onto the floor. "One demerit!" With a flourish, Cohen made a big X.

"Look at this floor," said Flinn, forcing Norman down under the bed, and rubbing his hand in the dust.

"Floors," announced Cohen, marking the book. "One demerit."

"This tent's a shit house!" shouted Flinn. "Tannenbaum, another inspection like this, and it'll mean no movies and no canteen! Now tell your campers what they did wrong."

"But you just told them," said Sid, helping Norm brush the dust off his legs.

"I was talking to you, not to them."

"They still heard you." Sid looked at him. "You know, friend, you got a pretty loud voice."

Cohen dropped his pencil. Flinn just stared.

The Great White Father marched up the steps. Cohen reeled off the list. Steiner's eyes closed to slits, the way Japs looked when they were about to take aim, his jaw jutting out, his face stern. Sid Tannenbaum stood there as if he didn't know what it was all about, like a rookie. Maybe he should never have hired him.

Sid looked into Steiner's beady eyes. Maybe he should never have come.

BASIC TRAINING

PRESTON CHECKED HIS RACQUET. It was an old one, strung and restrung. The gut was bright and lustrous. The wood was scratched and nicked, but still serviceable, more than that—still good, still bearing the sprawling autograph, Jay T. Preston. It was an old signature, written when his name on a racquet made it a big seller. Now his signature was small and compressed. No manufacturer would think of using it. Because he was old, forgotten, an ex-champ.

Every counselor a champion. That was Steiner's motto. That's why he'd picked him over the others, younger men, not only younger, but Jewish, "their own kind." If it weren't for the films, he might never have gotten the job.

Year after year he watched them; winters, in the club at St. Petersburg, summers, at Omongo. As if he was seeing himself for the first time, the young Jay Preston scoring at Wimbledon, the young Jay Preston winning at Forest Hills, the old Jay Preston in an empty social hall, clubhouse, hotel room, sitting in front of a screen, watching someone he'd once known—himself.

[33]

Without the films, he might never have remembered that once he'd been on top of the world, that once, long ago, he'd been hailed by thousands of people, people now too busy watching someone else, in real action on real tennis courts, to think of the old Jay T. Preston from way back, now only an emulsion of silver nitrate on a spliced and sutured strip of celluloid.

The new boys wouldn't even have seen the films. He'd have to start all over again, dropping a word here, a phrase there, casually, until they found out they were dealing with the former tennis champion of the United States. He'd see the change then, the respect, the sudden awe, the eager questions, the timid requests for his autograph.

Preston wound the key on the canister. He liked to hear the hiss of air, to feel the softness of the new balls as they tumbled out, to see them bounce, young, full of life. Jay T. Preston knew something which he'd never told anyone. You might call it a secret, a secret he didn't dare reveal because if he did they'd call him a crank. It was this: some-day all the other champs—the Olympic stars, the Rose Bowl linemen, the bright-eyed Wimbledonians, the cocky, brawny winners—someday, though they didn't know it, though they didn't even think about it, someday they'd be like Jay T. Preston, an illegible signature on a tarnished trophy, in the dusty corner of an empty room.

"Kids," said Preston, "I'm going to reverse the pro-cedure a little. Instead of starting with the beginners, I'm going to work on the back-hand stroke with the old-timers. You new boys can slap the ball around for a while. Get the feel of your racquets."

"Let's keep score, Norm," shouted Randy.

"I don't know how."

"I don't, either. The hell with it. Let's just have fun."

They were both crummy, but it didn't matter. Here,

you could relax. No one cared. No one was keeping score. Winning and losing here were the same thing.

The morning sun felt good. He missed. Norm smiled. Randy shrugged his shoulders. Even Norm seemed to be having fun for a change. Maybe it was the noise of the strings against the ball that he liked. It was as if they, Norm and him, were playing a tune, as if they were holding banjos. Pang. Pung. Pang. Pung. Just the sounds were good. And the sun, too, and the weight of his tennis banjo. And Norm, smiling, finally smiling . . .

Lieutenant Flinn turned on them, as if searching for a spy. "Any of you guys think we're here to monkey around, get this straight: we mean business." Flinn was tough. You had to say that for him.

"Your life is at stake on this firing range. All that keeps us from being another punk nation is the power of our guns. And if we're going to be strong, then it's guys like you, training to shoot on a little rifle range like this, who'll keep us strong."

"You ever shoot before?" Randy whispered across Mel to Norman.

"No talking on the firing range," shouted Flinn. "That's the rule around here."

Norman reached for his fifth bullet. He looked under the mattress. Nothing but empty cartridges. Maybe he'd already fired it.

Flinn was examining the targets. "Where in God's name is your last bullet?"

Norman shrugged. "You only gave me four."

"Listen, buddy, I counted them out myself."

"That really takes the cake," said Mel. "I can just see him aiming at somebody else's target."

"What a jerk," said Mike.

Flinn was mad. He looked as if he'd take the gun and use it on him. The kids crowded around, ready for a good fight. "Four," yelled Greenberg, holding up four fingers, "that's all you gave me." Flinn made a fist. The bugle.

"If I catch you lying again," cried Flinn, "I'll . . ."

They marched to the arts and crafts shop.

It was like playing in a mud pile. Randy had thought clay was colored, like the stuff you bought in the store. But this was dirty and messy, like the bay when the tide went out.

"To me, it's just plain old stupid," grumbled Norman.

"Hey, teach, I need help." Mike was forming a long coil, like a constipated stool. Fat Stuff Halpern made a giant candy bar. Mel aimed a brown snowball at Randy. Norm added flowery nipples to a pair of life-sized breasts.

Sid Tannenbaum stared out the window. His parents were still mad at him for choosing Alfred College. "Cheap trade school," said his mother.

"Not so cheap," said his father. "How about Queens College? You could take accounting. Handicrafts? That's for old maids."

"A hobby we can understand," said his mother. "Your father loves fishing, but does he need to learn it in college? Where would we be if he spent every day at some brook?"

"Eating herring," said his father. "Sidney, let's get down to earth. College is expensive, and I'm not paying for daydreams." So he'd lied, told them he'd become a ceramics engineer, and Alfred was the only college in the East with that course.

"What are you, a bunch of juvenile delinquents?" screamed Sid, as Mike's phallic clay pile raped Norm's pin-up bosom. Mel's snowball overshot, and went out the door.

Steiner stomped in, the clay dripping down his shoulder. "This is what I'm paying for?" he demanded, holding the scrapings under Tannebaum's face.

Sid nodded. "It's darn good clay, sir."

"It ought to be; I paid enough for it," snapped the Great White Father. "That's why I don't want to see it wasted," he concluded, wiping his fingers.

"I'm trying to teach them to use their hands," explained Sid, enthusiastically. "So later on they won't have to depend on the wheel."

"You mean after all the money I spent on those wheels?" The boys reshaped their work quickly, breasts into bowls, asses into ashtrays.

"Tannenbaum," the Great White Father refused to look at their clay piles, "there doesn't seem to be any organization around here."

"That's because they're progressing at their own speed, sir," said Sid, his eyes afire. "That's how we bring out their creativity, the good they've got in their fingers."

"Philosophy's all right for the classroom," said Steiner. "But this is real life. I'm setting up a contest for the best Intermediate pottery. I'll announce the rules tomorrow."

Sid started to say something. Steiner about-faced sharply, like a well-trained soldier, and marched out.

TENDING THE HOME FIRES

STEINER CLICKED ON the fluorescent lamp. He examined the schedule. The clock struck. He checked his chronometer. Perfectly synchronized.

A knock. Lieutenant Flinn. Steiner smiled. He liked talking to counselors. With the campers you never knew: were you the boss or were they?

Flinn stood rigid, at attention: "It's about Greenberg, sir."

Steiner opened a desk drawer. "Have a cigarette."

"Thank you, sir, I don't smoke."

"Good idea," said Steiner. "Self-discipline, that's the thing."

"You told me if I had any special problems with him to see you, sir." He felt like a newlywed, asking the doctor for advice.

Steiner's headache was getting worse. He should have shouted for Sylvia to bring him some aspirins. "Now this Greenberg," said Steiner. "I don't like to make a special case out of him. But I don't want him complaining to his parents, either. Do you understand me?"

"Yes," said Flinn, "I do, sir."

Steiner stuck out his fist. "I train these boys to be strong, Lieutenant, to live in a world where dog eats dog." He drew his chair closer. "But the parents want their children to be weak like them. Strength scares them. They want their children to go through some empty rituals they call prayer rather than stand on their own two feet."

"Don't you think, sir," said Flinn, looking at Steiner, testing his reaction, "that maybe it's, well . . . a Jewish trait?"

"Of course it is. Exactly. Why do you think I keep that rabbi, Yeslin, here? Because they're going to learn something from his singsong? I hired him so Aunt Minnie won't think they're sending her little nephew to a camp for goyim. Take Preston, the tennis champ. I practically had to sneak him in. I couldn't get a Jewish coach half as good."

"Sir, I like you and what you're doing." Flinn looked at him squarely. "I like you because you're an American before, well . . ." Was he talking too much? Was he too far ahead, out where it was dangerous?

"Say it, Lieutenant. Speak freely."

"Well, sir, you're not just a Jew, you're an American."

"Of course I'm an American first," said Steiner. His headache was worse.

"I can just see that Greenberg kid complaining what an ogre his rifle counselor is." Flinn smiled.

"You mean he's written home!" Steiner jumped up.

"No, no, sir, I was just talking."

"Well, let it be talk. I'll take a look at his letters before I post them." He watched Flinn's eyes. Some counselors wouldn't like that. "Once in a while I censor the letters. Like in the military. You understand." Flinn's face remained immobile, obedient. He was all right, that man.

"Lieutenant, I'm going to tell you something. Omongo is in trouble."

"What do you mean?"

"Money. We're in the red. I have to make a decision. You know Oronsky?"

"The one in the same tent with Greenberg?"

"His father. Wealthy man. Dress business. He's offered to buy me out. He'll retain me as acting head. But I'll be powerless, completely powerless. Not because Oronsky's stronger or because he has higher principles than me. It's because he has more money. Strip away his bankroll and what is he? Put him in Omongo to fight it out for himself, and where would a man like Oronsky be?"

"Maybe that's why he sends his son here," said Flinn. "He knows that when the chips are down, the only thing that counts is brute strength."

"You're like me," said Steiner. "An idealist."

Flinn's face glowed as if kindled by an inner light. "You know, I didn't think I'd like Omongo at first. I'll be perfectly frank, sir, if it's O.K. with you."

"Go ahead," said Steiner. "Sometimes I like people who talk openly."

"I thought Omongo would be just another camp. But

[39]

it's not. Mr. Steiner, you've really got something. Why, Omongo should be twelve months a year!"

Steiner lit another cigarette. "Only one person can save us. Mrs. Greenberg, Norman's mother. Splendid woman. I suggested she might establish a foundation in her name. Tax deduction, you know."

Flinn nodded.

"I've got a splitting headache."

"Sorry to hear that, sir. Can I get you an aspirin?"

"Two," said Steiner. "I'm all tied up with work here. Upstairs. Just ask Sylvia."

Steiner went back to his schedule. With all the talk about the Spartan life and discipline, he had to admit he liked to be waited on. It was almost a necessity.

Flinn knocked. "I came for some aspirins for your husband."

"Wait a minute. I'll get some things on."

Flinn leaned against the wall. A crystal chandelier hung in the stairwell. The hallway was carpeted with thick velvet. Some setup. All that talk about not enough money. Steiner must draw some salary. Of course, that's why Omongo was going broke. The counselors certainly weren't getting it.

The door opened. Flinn snapped to attention. She was wearing a thin negligee, a sort of kimono. She looked older than when he'd first met her. No make-up, maybe that's why. Her lips were cracked. Her skin was rough, like a man's. Under her nose was a wisp of peach fuzz. Her kimono fell open for a split second, revealing her breasts, hanging down like overripe malignant melons.

"I haven't seen you around very much, Mrs. Steiner," said Flinn, trying to be polite.

She pointed to her easel. "I've been busy."

Flinn marched to the canvas. "Looks pretty good."

" 'Pretty good'?" She laughed. "Well, you look pretty good, too."

[40]

"What's that?"

"I said you look as if being here agrees with you."

"It does," he said briskly. Where in God's name were the aspirins?

"I guess you're as busy with your guns and all that, as I am with my painting."

"I guess so."

"Why are you so nervous?"

"Nervous?"

"Yes, what are you looking for?"

"The aspirins. Didn't I tell you?"

"I thought you were here on a social call."

Flinn drew himself to attention. "You husband sent me. He has a terrible headache."

"That *is* too bad." She was smiling. "When is your wife coming for a visit, Lieutenant?"

"I'm not married." The shelves, the bureau, the night table—where were they?

She stepped to the bathroom. "He won't ever get up to find them for himself," she muttered.

"He's too busy," explained Flinn. "Too busy to think about such small things."

"Is that it?" She emerged from the bathroom. She placed the aspirins in his palm.

He jerked his hand away. "I have to go," he mumbled.

"I hope we'll see more of each other, Lieutenant." He rushed toward the closet. "No," she laughed, "it's this way."

She led him to the door. "Drop in again," she suggested. "Any time."

He ran down the stairs.

BATTLE MOCK-UP

||||||||||||||||||||||||||||||||||||||||||||||||||||||||||||

"THERE USED TO BE INDIANS all over this place," said Randy. "That's what Eagle told me."

Mike folded the page where the Jungle Queen was being raped by two hairy gorillas. "Eagle's half nigger. That's why he's so stupid."

Fat Stuff tossed a candy wrapper under the bed. "Woo, woo," he chanted, putting two fingers behind his head for feathers. "Me Big-um Chief Sitting Eagle."

"Big Chief Shitting Eagle," smiled Mel, drawing a ghostly hand under Wonder Woman's chastity belt.

"Tent Thirty-eight, lights out!" shouted a counselor.

"Where the heck's our Uncle Sid," said Mike.

"Probably goofing off in arts and crafts," said Norman.

"Ain't that sweet," said Mike. "Hey, Mel, you're Sid and I'm coming at you with my giant baseball bat. I'm going to break your itty-bitty vase in two." He grabbed a pillow.

"Leave my precious vase alone," said Mel in a girl's voice. "You cwack my vase and I'll thmash you."

Mike wasn't joking. His pillow knocked Mel to the floor. Norman's pillow slapped Mike in the face.

"Dirty!" cried Mike. "I wasn't ready." Randy hit Oronsky. Mike hit back. It spread like a disease from one tent to the next, with feathers flying, pillows crashing. With yells and battle cries. Even the counselors joined in, at first as if they were trying to break it up, then for the fun of it, with all their might, with all their hate.

Rabbi Yeslin ran among the tents like a nervous usher at a children's matinée. "Boys," he cried, "let's have no roughhousing. We don't want no hoodlums here." A pillow struck from out of the dark.

Steiner marched to the battleground. The Great White Father! They dropped their pillows. Not a sound. "Order," commanded the Great White Peacemaker, puffing on his pipe.

Obediently, they marched to the Parade Grounds, carrying their pillows, stacking them like pieces of captured ammunition. Steiner supervised the disarmament. Boys would be boys and he expected this once every year. It showed they had fighting spirit. If it didn't happen, something was wrong.

"But don't let it happen again," he warned the contrite assembly, his voice suddenly gloomy. "It's too expensive."

THE CHAPLAIN

RABBI YESLIN HAD SPENT at least a half-dozen summers away from Brooklyn. He'd been cantor at a kosher hotel in the Catskills. But his voice had failed. It was no longer loud and plaintive. He was getting older, his hair grayer, his teeth more rotten. It had come to this: a rabbi in a camp for Reform Jews.

Steiner was getting a bargain. Nowadays to earn his

living he had to be a bargain, to cut prices, to close his eyes, to say everything in English. That's the way it went. What could you do?

Long ago—it seemed like a hundred years—his tiny congregation had disappeared to the suburbs and his temple had become a deserted island in a sea of Puerto Ricans. The president of the synagogue had made a bad investment, the mortgage couldn't be met, and the temple had to be sold. Sold! To a syndicate who turned it into a supermarket, with stained glass for windows, and an altar for a meat block, piled with bacon, pork, pigs' feet! Times were changing, moving, like a hurricane.

He tried to bend with the wind. Anything, just to make a living: blessing the dead in a Long Island cemetery, until they found someone who could speak English better; cutting foreskins, until they replaced him with a gentile doctor wearing a big cross; blessing salami, until the Union of Orthodox Rabbis forced him out.

He copied speeches from an old book and sold them for bar mitzvahs, but they were too flowery, too fancy. No one understood them. What could he say—that they weren't even his?

He tried being a marriage broker, operating as a free lance from his little apartment, but his lists grew smaller, the good girls fewer. Nowadays, men wanted a special type, the kind you found late at night, alone in a delicatessen, waiting. He had to draw the line somewhere. Marriages, yes, but "trial marriages," never! No trials; he was no lawyer.

He became a professional mourner for a small-time burial society. He was good at it, one of the best. But times caught up with him again. Business fell off. People wanted a quick burial, efficient. No candles, no mourners, no words. One, two, three, and into the pit.

That's how it went. No more yamilkes, no more tallis

shawls, no more Hebrew, no more jobs. He pitied the rabbis of the future: how would they ever make a living? They wouldn't even look like Jews. They'd make their noses over like movie stars; they'd trade in their Hanukkah for harmonicas; their matzos for martinis; their Bibles for bacon. Maybe his brother was right to go into law.

And yet, when it was all over, when his day's earnings were counted and put into the little brown box, there was still something to be said for being a rabbi. There was something about reciting a prayer, about fingering the tallis, about being a Jew. That counted for something, too. Money wasn't everything.

He'd make out. Somehow. Maybe the Puerto Ricans would move back where they came from, maybe the congregation would return. They promised never to forget Jerusalem. Maybe they'd remember Bensonhurst, too. He would wait.

Meanwhile, it got embarrassing. Always the comparisons with his brother Morris. Morris' split-level colonial, his green car, his twenty-four-inch television. His three sons, his two-week Miami vacations, his full-length mink for his wife.

Why hide it? Beneath all the words and prayers, he was jealous. How could he call himself a rabbi? A rabbi had a congregation, he was looked up to. Who looked up to him? God, he used to say. But God looked down. All he could do was go on complaining, and hope for the best.

Rabbi Yeslin stood at the microphone. Behind him was the pile of torn and dirty pillows. Before him stood the hungry campers, stiff, like trees. What was he going to say?

"Fellow tribesmen of Omongo." Steiner smiled. A page out of his own book. The old rabbi was trying to fit himself in.

"This is the first of what I sincerely hope will be a long and profitable series of talks on certain moral aspects of our religion. It takes faith in Judaism to win: this is what I want to discuss with you this morning."

Two hundred campers were playing the shift-your-weight game, trying to endure the torrent of words. Flinn looked at his watch. He focused his eyes on the rabbi's bald spot.

"Just as you must fight with all your might to win a game, so you must be religious with all your might to win a successful life. In the last run, it is God who determines who will be a winner and who a failure. It is God who decides which baseball player will hit the home run, which lawyer will win the case, which camper will get the silver trophy.

"On what basis does God decide? On the basis of who can run the fastest? On the basis of who has the most muscles, or who is the most clever? No, fellow tribesmen, God does not depend on such small things to make His decision.

"God awards those who believe in God. God awards those who pray to God. God awards those whose knees are bent, not at a baseball plate, but at His altar, in His service, at His command."

"What a Yid," whispered Flinn. Steiner shrugged. What could he do? The parents wanted it. And they were getting it.

"God says unto you, *Sh'ma Yisroel Adonoi Elohenu Adonoi Echod . . .*'"

The campers shifted to the other leg.

"You who have had the honor of performing the bar mitzvah know how important these words are. You who are still too young will soon discover their meaning."

Steiner looked at his chronometer. "I'll tell the dining hall we're a little late," he whispered. Flinn nodded. Steiner slipped away. Flinn aimed his imaginary rifle, the one he

[46]

always carried with him. Ping! Right at the bald spot. The rabbi crumbled to the ground. God laughed.

"Many of your parents are content to give you no religious education at all," the rabbi continued indignantly. "They turn you into the world ignorant and helpless, helpless against the power of Almighty God."

Randy shifted to his left foot. There was no escape. At home, he could run from his father's lectures to the bay. At school, he drew pictures in the margin of his book. But here he was trapped. It was like a stupid love scene in a good war picture, when all the kids got restless and started clapping hands, stamping on the floor, while the lovers hugged and whispered the same darn words, over and over.

He counted the stones at his feet, four, five, six, as if he were saying a prayer. Like the rabbi, talking about something no one ever listened to except old people. And *they* only made believe. It was their way of counting stones. It was like his bar mitzvah last winter, the same dopey thing, with his Uncle Nathan asking, "How does it feel to be thirteen, to be a man?"

"Don't rush things, Nathan," said his mother. "He's not a man yet. Wait for the service."

He didn't even understand the words. "Hebrew, it's a religious language," his mother told him. "A sacred language. English—what's that?"

"English!" his father said. "A newcomer. Hebrew's the oldest known language in the world. Positively the oldest."

The local synagogue wasn't good enough. They'd gone to another one, way at the end of the Bronx, to a place with some class.

"What a beautiful architecture," said his Uncle Nathan. "Look at them carvings. Pure gold. Don't you think it's nice, Jake?"

"I should imagine so," said his father. "This temple,

Natie, is strictly the best. People come from the Grand Concourse to attend."

Randy went back of the altar to a little room where the old rabbi was waiting. "Don't be nervous. Between you and me, if you miss a couple of lines, they'll never know the difference. And neither will the good Lord." The rabbi smiled, as if it was a kind of private joke.

"What a fancy temple," said a cousin, her simulated pearls drooping. "It must be costing the Levines a pretty penny."

"How much?" asked Natie.

Only his mother noticed Randy, a sheep being led to the altar. The old rabbi, with a slow, pontifical movement, opened the Bible. He looked up with beneficence.

"Not so nervous," said his mother in a loud stage whisper. "They can all see." No one saw.

"I wonder what it cost the Levines for that spread downstairs. I hear they spent everything they had."

"So generous they are."

"Personally, I think they live beyond their means."

"What is Jake, a factory worker?"

"No, I hear he's a foreman."

"So how much could a guy like that make, four, five thousand?"

"You think that's all? Then how does he come to a temple like Rodeph Sholom?"

Just how much *was* this costing, wondered Mr. Levine. He'd totaled the bills at home, but now he'd forgotten. It was a lot of money, anyhow. It made him sweat just to think about it. Why didn't they open one of the windows? "To My Darling Husband Henry Cohen." "To My Dearest Daughter Sonia Metarski." How colorful, green and purple and orange, like so many spring garments. He wondered if he'd ever have enough to buy one of those for himself. "To The Loving Memory Of Our Beloved Jacob

[48]

Levine, Dearest Husband Of Esther, Darling Father Of Randy." It wouldn't look right, buying a window for himself. *She'd* get the glass. Him? He'd be lucky to get a window in B'nai Beth Yaakov—a cheap-looking pane in a second-class synagogue.

Mrs. Levine sat back in her pew, contented. What an expensive rabbi! So distinguished, so fine. She thought of the surprise waiting downstairs. Sterngluck Brothers, the classiest caterers in the Bronx. How they cost!

But who could think of pennies, at a time like this? The bar mitzvah of her son. Her one and only loving son. It was the highpoint in her life.

No, there'd be others. He'd get married, and that'd be a highpoint, too. He'd have a child, and that would be a highpoint. Another child, another highpoint. Then the sons would have bar mitzvahs, and each would be a highpoint. Then the highpoints would be over. She'd be old. She'd pass away. She looked at the windows. How pretty. Especially that pink and purple one. Would Jake care enough to buy a whole window? It would certainly cost a lot. It would be the final highpoint in her life.

The cantor was singing. They remembered the old days. Good enough to be at the Metropolitan, thought Mrs. Bronson. Mr. Bronson preferred Gilbert and Sullivan. Natie thought he had a frog in his throat, but that was how all cantors sounded, sad, melancholy. Frog or no frog, they liked it. They were children again, listening to a sweet and tender lullaby. They gazed at the memorial windows. They wanted to cry.

But the singing went on and on. They were getting hungry. Mrs. Bronson had heard the latest rumor—squab. They'd probably have candied sweet potatoes and baby green peas. Too much starch. But wasn't this a special event?

Mrs. Haimovitz was filling her plate with moist, heavy

gefilte fish, with tingling pirogen, with dainty kreplach. They were whispering and nudging each other.

Mrs. Levine, in the front row, turned around and ordered them with a frown to keep quite please, it was almost over. All she got were a few waves and some thrown kisses.

The cantor gave up. Everyone sighed with relief. The tuning of the violin worked its way up from the Green Room. They must have eaten already. Maybe they were munching now, in between notes.

Randy stepped forward. Mrs. Levine stood up with her loudest hush, please. She signaled for Randy to begin.

"Dearest, beloved parents. Beloved relatives. Kind guests. On this day. On this sacred and holy day. On this revered and always-to-be-remembered day. I am, by Jewish law and tradition, a man."

"What a fine beginning," whispered Jake, as if he hadn't heard the speech at home, rehearsed a thousand times until it came out of his ears.

"Shh!" said Mrs. Levine, enjoying this highpoint. She nodded for him to go on. Randy paused. He continued to pause. She stepped down from her highpoint, in a wave of panic. She'd forgotten the next line herself.

"It is to my parents. It is to my dearest, beloved parents who I owe everything." She relaxed. Truly a highpoint.

"Without them I would not be the Jew I am. It was their firm yet understanding upbringing, it was their kindness and their holiness and their love-of-God, which has taught me respect, which has taught me to treasure the beautiful things in life: to give generously to the temple, to give from the heart rather than from the pocket."

Jake sighed with relief. What a long sentence!

"Wonderful!" exclaimed Mrs. Bernstein.

"You mean he memorized it?" said a cousin. "You mean to tell me he's not looking?"

The speech was over. Randy stepped down from the

[50]

platform. A squadron of aunts surrounded him, kissing and hugging. He felt naked and exposed, as if he'd told a whopping lie.

"The truth of Jewish learning," continued Yeslin, as the campers shifted weight again, "must not die."

He explained how the customs and rituals of Jacob and David and Moses were being despoiled, profaned, ignored. Flinn looked at his watch. The schedule was in pieces, broken by that long-nosed rabbi, smashed by his long red tongue.

"Let us return to the truth of the past, to the religion of *Sh'ma Yisroel*." He pulled a black skullcap from his pocket and placed it on his bald spot. "I ask all of you to do the same." He waited.

They looked at the gravel. They looked at the flagpole. They looked at each other.

"If you have nothing else, then use a handkerchief."

One by one, campers and counselors began covering their heads. It was crazy. Fat Stuff didn't have a handkerchief. He pulled a crumpled candy wrapper from his pocket and dropped it on his head.

That broke the spell. Everyone started laughing. Even the woodpeckers and squirrels and grasshoppers. Yeslin looked on with horror.

Steiner switched to a tape-recording of the Marine Corps Band playing "The Stars and Stripes Forever."

The rabbi kept opening and closing his mouth. Steiner turned the volume higher. The Marine Corps Band drew nearer. The campers marched, their skullcap handkerchiefs perched on their heads.

"Thank God they shut him up," shouted Mel.

"Who, the rabbi with the rabies?" cried Randy.

"Hey, Levine, you ought to be on TV!" laughed Mike. Randy beamed, as if for the first time a spotlight had been thrown on him.

Fat Stuff Halpern waved the candy wrapper as he waddled along, making Jewish faces, shaking his head from side to side, moaning *oy-oy, oy-oy*. What a clown, what a terrific joker, the funniest guy in Omongo. Everyone laughed.

Randy turned away. Fat Stuff had stolen his show.

INDEPENDENCE DAY

||||||||||||||||||||||||||||||||||||||||||||||||||||||||||||||

A BLAZING ROCKET flew into the black sky, smaller and smaller, until it was a fiery dot, another star in a swarm of galaxies, staring down on the summer-evening ritual celebrating a moment, long ago on the fourth day of July, when wigged and black-cloaked figures had declared to the universe that they were free.

Cohen and Gans scurried down the pier. A spark traveled along the winding fuse. Flinn stood over it, a witch over her brew, face straining, hands trembling; stood there till the last second. Then, just before the explosion, he ran along the pier, his face covered with terror.

A burst of blue, white, yellow, then darkness. Another burst, a whole cosmos of planets and fiery comets. The campers, strung safely along the Parade Grounds, applauded.

They worked feverishly. The kids wanted everything to be one-two-three, the way it was in war pictures. That's what it was to them, Steiner versus the counselors.

A brilliant magnesium fire lit up Steiner's platform across the lake, the pier, the Parade Grounds, the two hundred campers rising in a body, witnessing a sneak attack.

"Damn it!" cried Flinn. "He knows his flares aren't supposed to go off till we've set ours."

"Let's have a little fun," said Gans. "We'll show the old fox we can beat him."

They lit the fuse. Cohen ran. He was sweating. He felt sick. He fell into the soft, safe grass.

Gans walked, swinging his arms. As if, without a doubt, he'd come in first, that he was just what everyone said he was—a champ, a born champ.

And crazy Flinn! Still standing there. That bastard, he'd be burned to death. What was he trying to prove?

SWOOSH. Roman candles. Flinn ran for all he was worth. Just in time. "You O.K.?" cried Cohen.

"I could have stayed there longer."

"Sure," smiled Cohen.

"I didn't want to get you old ladies all nerved up."

Gans snickered.

Sylvia Steiner sat on the porch, watching. The colored streamers were quite beautiful. They had an abstract quality like the fire and smoke of the Valkyries riding furious steeds across the stage. The explosions were drums booming in the orchestra pit. The glow, like a hundred klieg lights high in the wings, was at once real and unreal, explosive and foolish, absurd and entertaining.

The last flicker died away. The cheering campers, the Parade Grounds, the trees faded into the night. The act was over. The yellow porch bulb glowed faintly, casting its pall over her face and body. A tired yellow, the yellow of old newspapers, ghastly, the color of disease, old age, dying. Not Van Gogh's yellow, with his blazing sun, his flaming flowers and fiery fields—life burning itself out, destroying itself, feeding on its own heat. That's what he'd tried to paint: the flames, the burning out, the self-destruction which was living.

[53]

She'd tried it too, skyscrapers, whole cities burning on her canvas. Then the questions. What was it? What did it (she hated the word) represent?

They were too abstract, too filled with energy. Life was too much for them. It had been too much for her, too, that daily torture at the stake. Her style changed. The leaves turned green again. The red rivers cooled into a comforting blue. The hot orange cities froze into concrete gray. The sky, those churning crimson skies of hers, became azure, filled with fat, fleecy clouds, like so many pillows. No, they nodded, she hadn't lost her touch after all. That was much better. They were with her again, her friends, her critics, nodding, approving, compliments, praise. She preferred it.

Another onslaught of rockets, this time from her husband, on the cliffs, like Wotan himself. She could picture him, every revolting detail: his eyes measuring their height; his smile measuring their success; his fingers tapping impatiently, anxious to set off more rockets, higher ones, brighter.

"A step backwards." That's what he'd said. For three years she'd slept with him, paid him. Didn't it mean anything that her pictures were accepted again, that she was a success again? An "idealist," he called himself. He was as bought off as any other man. Wasn't the money she gave him a bribe, a bribe to love? Why not?

It was all a matter of buying and selling. Even Van Goghs were bought and sold like so many dozen eggs. They had a market value like everything else. Everything, everyone was for sale, on the auction block, displaying limbs and breasts, hurriedly dabbing lipstick and mascara, perfumes and lotions. The art business was no different.

That's what it was—a business. With fads: a fad for Van Gogh, a fad for Renoir, a fad for Picasso. It was a matter of who you knew, of what contacts you had, of what cocktail parties you attended, of whether or not you were with it, the fad, obedient, faithful.

More fireworks. It was a production, a masterpiece, one burst after another, red, green, yellow. He'd never be outdone, not Harry Steiner.

The boys were on their feet, cheering. The yells and explosions were deafening. The light of the flares was blinding. All so they'd be entertained, so they'd return next year, pouring their money into the cash register. All this sound and fury so that next year she could buy herself a bigger sofa, another lover, a newer mink.

Flinn arranged rockets, candles, cherry bombs, flares, a cosmic designer, a creator of stars and planets, God about to strike His match. The holy spark crawled up the fuse, toward the solemn rows of pyramids, prisms, spheres. The stars and stripes rose like a protective canopy, swelling into patriotic reds, whites, blues. Flinn got up, as if to bow. His grand finale would make the Great White Father's contraptions across the lake look like miserable, cheap toys.

He walked to the edge of the pier. Steiner's turn now. Just let him try.

A blaze of light, a chaos of rocks bouncing like tennis balls, as if a volcano had erupted, as if the whole world were being sucked in and spit out in a single, catastrophic vomit. Then the echoing roar, again and again, like a monster shouting obscenities across a burned and gutted earth.

Flinn pounded his fists against the wooden slats. "No fair. Dynamite!" The campers cheered. Taps sang out jubilantly from the loudspeaker. "No fair! Listen! He used dynamite!" The bugle played a loud, triumphant fanfare, a chorus of victory, Steiner's, Steiner's.

A. W. O. L.

IT WAS ALMOST TIME to close the gateway. A few more counselors would be sneaking by. He'd let them go, too. He wasn't a policeman, not at his pay. Did Steiner think because he was an Indian he'd make a good lookout? It was them crazy movies.

Eagle's eyes peered from their deep sockets. A couple of months and they'd all be gone. He'd have Omongo to himself. Winter. Then it too would go, the cold and the snow, because he'd been too strong.

The sun would come out and it'd be nice again, leaves, flowers, birds again. Then them: Steiner and his two hundred Jews, yelling, screaming, coming back like locusts. And Steiner would slip him a ten-dollar bill the very first day, same as always, putting it in his hand like a secret. He'd tell him to get things all fixed up, and he'd talk to him about putting in a new windowpane, a new screen door, and how to do it carefully like he was a little boy who didn't understand if he didn't hear it two or three times. Like when he had to sell the place, because all the taxes were hanging over him. This fat Jew man came up from New York and counted the money into his hand, like he didn't deserve it.

Nothing was his any more, except his broken-down house. The man from New York hired him at a dollar a day. The next year, thirty Jews came up; and the next year, sixty; then in the hundreds. And Steiner telling him to chop down the last tree near the lake, so they'd have room for another flagpole. That tree was big when he was a boy, big when his father was a boy. It'd be a stump, and Steiner'd give him a dollar to cut it.

All the trees, waiting to be cut down for dollar bills. His trees. The animals, too, the foxes and rabbits and deer. All hiding behind the bushes waiting for the two hundred Jews to leave. Then they'd come out, sometimes even a deer, right outside his house, and he'd step out and shoot it. You could like animals, because all you had to do was step outside and aim; you didn't have to sit there waiting, like for them two hundred Jews, waiting for them to go, hating them all summer long.

Noisy shoes scraping against the gravel. This one wouldn't have a pass, either. Only the nurse and cooks could go tonight. If others went, he was supposed to tell. But the dimes and quarters kept him quiet. Those little extras. Like all that money he made sneaking in candy for the fat boy.

He'd save the extra money and buy groceries for winter. When they were gone he'd get drunk. He'd run through the kitchen and sit in the Mess Hall, like a Jew, holding a knife and fork in the air and yelling at the cooks. He'd imagine someone coming out, and he'd tell them to take it back, like a Jew: "Not cooked right!" He'd take another drink, break into the bathroom, and sit on the white stone toilet bowl like a Jew. He'd take a crap and curse like a Jew because the handle wouldn't bring any water. He'd take another drink and run down to the lake, all his; he'd run across the bare ground which was once covered with trees and was all his. The lake, the trails and the woods, and that tree in the Parade Grounds were his, not Steiner's.

"Here's a half-buck." Flinn grinned at him.

Eagle pointed to the open gate. He spit a wad of tobacco juice. "Come back, you dirty robber," he yelled, looking at the coin in his withered fist. "Come back, liar. Damn Jew. You only gave me a quarter."

Inside the tavern, the tubes of the chromium juke box flashed, ready to go. One hundred tunes, 10¢ a play, 3 for 25. One section was titled "Down Memory Lane," but Flinn was in no mood for nostalgia. Another was called "Westerns," a third "Sweet," and next to it, "Hot." The last group, a small one, featured Victor Herbert and Johann Strauss: "Classics." Something for every taste.

Flinn inserted a quarter. A Classic, a Sweet and a Hot. The juke box began to sing: "How Can I Love You When I Hate You, Baby?" Cohen and Gans tapped out the rhythm on the imitation marble. Flinn sat down stiffly in the leatherette seat.

"Relax," said Cohen.

"The race is over," said Gans. "Steiner and his dynamite won. What the hell, there's always tomorrow."

"You mean there's always tonight," smirked Cohen. "These babes I got lined up are terrific. Remember Marge from last year, Bud?"

"What are the others like?" asked Flinn.

"I haven't seen them yet. We're a million miles from nowhere, Lieutenant. You can't be too fussy."

"I can use a hump," moaned Gans.

"Last time I had a piece," said Cohen, "was so long ago it's ancient history."

The Sweet ended. The Classic was spinning. "Kiss Me Till I Die." Based on Brahms.

"Who's getting Marge?" asked Gans. "I want to ride a horse I know's a winner."

Cohen looked up. "Why don't we let her decide? She's old enough to vote."

"What's she look like?" asked Flinn.

"Wait till you see," said Gans, shaping a pair of huge breasts and gigantic buttocks.

[58]

The record machine stopped. The tubes blinked.

"Hell," cried Flinn. "I got another coming." He called the waitress. "I put in a quarter and only got two plays," he whined.

"Tell it to the bartender. I got nothing to do with it."

A tall girl stood in the doorway, her round face reflecting the scarlet glow of the juke box. The bartender seemed to know her. They chatted. He bought her a beer.

Cohen and Gans were still at it. "Flip a coin," said Cohen. "Winner gets his pick."

Flinn stared at the frumpy blonde drinking beer. She stared back with her big painted eyes, her full-moon face, her puffed-up, painted lips. That was her? Flinn swallowed his whiskey.

"If you want Marge so much, take her," said Cohen. "To me, one's as good as another, so long as they ain't smelly."

Flinn gulped the last of his drink. It burned like a mouth wash, cleansing, purifying. He'd be kissing her, a dirty whore, her tongue darting in, catching hold of his, gripping it like a hook, in a diseased, odorous kiss. He tilted the glass way back to get a last taste of the disinfectant.

She'd finished her second. She was getting up. She stood among the scarlet rays, burning like a witch. She looked around, not seeing them. She stepped toward the door. Her eyes caught his. She smiled. Flinn twitched.

"Bob! Hey, Bob," she yelled across the room.

"Why don't we order another round," said Flinn loudly, trying to drown out her shrill voice.

Like a streetwalker, she strutted across the crowded room, with an ugly, dirty leer. She plopped down next to Flinn, her large body touching, her animal heat seeping through her skirt, her moist arms rubbing against his elbow.

"Marge, you know Bud. Bud Gans."

"Sure do," she winked. "Quite a man."

[59]

"I want you to meet another counselor, Lieutenant James Flinn."

"Lieutenant?" she arched her eyebrows. "I'm not used to meeting anything better than sergeants around here."

"Marine Reserves," snapped Flinn, as if answering a questionnaire.

"How about us getting the hell out," said Gans. "You can gab all you want later. Got your car, honey?"

The juke box was playing a Hot. "Electric-Chair Blues." As they passed, Flinn stuck his fingers in the return-coin slot.

Marge opened the apartment door. "It's not much, but here it is."

A knotty-pine bureau stood cater-cornered on a thread-bare Persian-style carpet. A painted Limoges-type dish dangled from the plaster wall near a five-and-dime reproduction of a Van Gogh "Sunflowers." Marge was planning to sell the knotty pine and go into Louis Fourteenth which was the latest thing, as soon as she got a few bucks together.

Gans tested the couch. "It's all right for us, honey. We're not used to any better." Actually his parents' "Sunflowers" was far superior. It had been manufactured by a new, expensive process which imitated the original right down to the very brush strokes. "Y'know, we got the same picture in our house."

"No kidding," said Cohen. "We do, too. It's in the kitchen."

"That yellow goes swell with the walls," said Marge.

Flinn said nothing. There were no pictures on the walls of his room. Not even religious ones.

"Say, Marge, did you know this character once cut off his ear for a girl?"

"I know," said Marge, popping a Chiclet down her throat. "That's why he used a hearing aid." They laughed.

[60]

"Don't think that's so funny," said Gans, looking prim. "His paintings sell for thousands of buckeroos."

"No kidding," said Marge. "I bet he makes a lot from picture rights."

"He's dead," said Gans.

"Oh, I'm sorry," said Marge.

"Let's not be so morbid," said Cohen. "What you got to drink?"

"Never mind the drinks," said Gans. "When are your friends coming?"

Flinn looked at Marge's subscription magazines. He picked up a month-old copy of *Sexology*. "You find anything new in that magazine?" Marge brushed her fingers across his hair. Flinn moved away. "Gee, he's a shy one, ain't he?" she sighed. "I like 'em that way, strong and silent."

The bell rang several times. "That's them." Marge got up. "I can tell from the way they ring. The first six notes of 'My Country 'Tis Of Thee.'"

"That's really clever," said Gans.

They knocked. The second stanza.

Marge opened the door. Flinn stood at attention.

"Hazel and Betty, I want you to meet a few friends of mine." They giggled.

Beasts! Flinn inched over to the corner. No better than Marge. Worse. Those guys would go for anything, long as it had an entrance way.

Marge turned on the radio. She and Gans started dancing. Cohen made time with Betty. They were looking at the sunflower picture. Cohen twisted his ear and offered it to her. Betty giggled.

Flinn picked up the magazine. "Are American Women Frigid?" "Whatcha reading?" Hazel snuggled next to him.

"It's not mine," cried Flinn. "I was just looking."

"I told Marge not to leave dirty books around the house," said Hazel. Her breasts were lopsided. Her breath smelled of Sen-Sen. Her lips were a hideous violet; her eyes were shrouded by long false eyelashes.

"That's a Van Gogh those kids were laughing at," she explained. "I got one, too. Only a copy, of course. The real McCoy costs hundreds."

"Hey, Hazel," yelled Betty, over Cohen's swaying shoulders. "This dance floor's pretty lonely." Cohen steered her to the switch. Without missing a beat, she flicked off the light. There were only two soft bulbs now, above a matched pair of porcelain figurines—French courtiers kissing the outstretched hands of painted ladies. Cohen was kissing Betty, rubbing his hands up and down the back of her neck. Flinn watched.

Hazel moved to get up. "I don't dance," said Flinn.

"Oh," she said. An embarrassed pause. "That's O.K. That's perfectly O.K. Betty once had a boy friend who didn't dance, either." Gans and Marge were locked in an embrace.

"Later on she dropped him."

Another pause. Hazel sat back. She let out a loud sigh. The painted courtiers were still kissing, the prim French ladies still looking the other way.

"You're older than they are," whispered Hazel. "I can tell. You're middle-aged, aren't you?"

Flinn said nothing.

"Your hands are cold as ice. Let's warm 'em." She took hold and kissed. Flinn jerked away, as if he'd been bitten.

"I have to go," he announced loudly.

"Bathroom's over there," purred Marge.

"I mean I'm leaving."

Everything stopped. "What's the trouble?" said Gans.

"It's not my fault," hollered Hazel. "I'm doing my share."

"The nerve," cried Betty. "What's he going to do, leave poor Hazel all alone?"

"Whatsa matter?" whispered Marge. "He married or something?"

"He's just putting on a big act," said Gans.

Marge clicked on the lights angrily. "Don't you like my girl friend?"

Hazel rose to her feet. "I never . . ."

"I don't want to talk about it," said Flinn.

"He's drunk," giggled Betty. "You guys been drinking too much. That's the trouble."

"Listen, girls," said Gans. "Go in the kitchen and we'll straighten this out."

"Never, in all my life . . ."

"Come on, Hazel." The girls marched into the kitchen.

"What's the trouble?" demanded Gans, his voice suddenly harsh. "Don't you like her?"

"She's a monster!" cried Flinn. "And I'm not screwing any monster."

"All right, if you're such a lousy sport," said Cohen, "take Betty."

"Take mine," said Gans. "Marge."

"No. They're all lousy."

"Shh! F' Christ's sake, tone it down."

Flinn edged toward the door. He could hear the girls arguing in the kitchen.

"You're scared, that's what it is," said Gans, drawing up close. "You're afraid to screw her."

"You're a damn liar," cried Flinn, making for the door. "You told me she'd be a knockout." He trotted down the stairs.

"Afraid," Gans shouted after him. "Scared of dames."

The girls ran to the doorway.

"He's leaving," shouted Marge.

"Never," shouted Hazel, "in all my life."

"Bastard!" shouted Betty.

"Stop him!" they cried.

SKIRMISH

|||||||||||||||||||||||||||||||||||||||||||||||||||||||||

THE TAXI DROVE OFF. Flinn stood in front of the gate, staring up at the commanding letters, OMONGO, silhouetted against the sky's eerie glow. Trees swarmed in from all sides. The sounds grew louder, Cohen and Gans shouting as he ran down the stairs, chanting from behind the rocks, over and and over: "Jamie is a sissy, is a sissy sissy sissy."

The animals, wild and savage, joined in with their bills, beaks, tongues, their pointed, poisonous fangs. A scream. Broken glass. Cheezit the cops.

In the cellar: "You're next. Don't chicken out." The whore, flat as a mattress. Surrounded by the gang. Fifteen, that's how old he was. The bare bulb. Everything so bright, so naked. "Turn it off."

"No," he cried. "You wanta get rolled?" They left it on.

She lay there on the blanket, stripped. They had to be fast.

The contest. The guy who comes fastest don't have to pay. He held out the watch, his dead father's watch. Everyone crowded around, pushing and shoving to get a better place. Ready. Go!

Up and at 'em. Over the top. Shouts. Clenched fists. Cheers. Going good, good, good. Finished!

"I can do better."

"You call that fast?"

Next one. Ready. Get set. The crowd closed in for the kill.

His turn up. His eyes closed. Pumping, pretending. "Look at 'im go. That's the best yet." Coming. Coming. Wowee! The record. He'd won. The champ. He wouldn't have to pay. In the bathroom, excited, alone, the lights out, his foster father snoring upstairs, he stood in front of the toilet . . .

The leaves rustled. The forest sounds became louder, more ferocious. He was afraid to run, to be chased, to be clawed to pieces.

He reached the Parade Grounds. The taunts, the screams ended. Was that why Steiner had cut the trees down, because he heard the noises, too? The only way to stop them was to tear down the whole damn forest, building street lights and sidewalks, filling them with cops. Omongo was a first step. And if they still heard it, then men would have to fight it out with each other, with bats, guns, spears, fighting to destroy the screams still lurking within them.

On the treeless plain he suddenly felt strong again. Boldly, he mounted the steps of the Great White Father's house. He was a champion, the victor, faster than anyone else by thirty-three seconds. Voices cheered him on. His medals rang against his chest.

FIRST FIRST FIRST FIRST

"Why didn't you knock!" Sylvia dropped her paintbrush. It was full of red.

He slammed the door. She stared at him, at his sharp, chiseled nose, his thin lips, at the hard body bulging beneath his light summer clothing.

He looked at the blinding bulb. He looked at the walls. No switch. He yanked off his shoe and struck it against the light. The room exploded into darkness. She laughed nervously. He pulled her toward him. He kissed her, firmly, his lips pressing not with tenderness, but with strength, passion-ate, intense. He started unbuttoning his shirt, finally ripping it off, flinging it to the floor, then dropping his trousers. He stood next to her, naked, touching. She started to pro-test: words, pleas, the old paraphernalia of love-making. He grabbed hold of her blouse and ripped it off. She stood, frozen. He pulled down her skirt. He threw her down. He jerked off her shoes, tossing them across the room.

"No," she muttered, turning her head, trying to avoid his angry kisses. "Not this way. Not on the floor."

Like a triumphant bull, he mounted. Once more, the darkness, the noises, creeping in from the forest, from out-side, crawling under the door, through the windows. *He couldn't do it. He hadn't come. He'd faked it. Then gone home and thought of his friends, their lust, their excitement. Not of the whore at all!*

It was the same now. Outside of her. Just like before. Thinking of *them.* Of Cohen and Gans, naked, in and out, in and out, their hard, animal panting, in-out, in-out, their white hot sperm shooting, splashing, spraying as he held her, tightening his ropelike arms, binding her to the floor.

His body twisted in a spasm. They were joined, torso to torso, by the glue, his glue, like something foul, mingling with her sweat, her blood, her cries, as she moaned, defeated, in pain.

He'd won.

MEDITATION

SID STEPPED ON THE TREADLE. The mound of clay spun, like a prayer wheel whispering incantations with each turn, a prayer of work, cyclical, repetitious, joyful: the work of farming with its slow-moving wheel of seasons; the work of spinning shuttles, churning bobbins; the tap, tap, tapping of hammers. Wasn't the world itself a wheel, whirling around, moon and planets, sun, even the whole universe, spinning with affirmation, generating heat, light, growth.

Slowly the vessel formed: the lip grew thinner; the neck, more fragile; the bottom, full and round. He inserted his forefinger into the vase's narrow opening and pressed. It was like giving birth, this subtle manipulation. No wonder people spoke of it as artistic *labor*. It brought forth the same anxieties as bearing a child, the same selflessness, intensity, the same pain.

With the potter's wheel you could see what you were making, giving shape, your own shape of yourself. With other machines, you gave of yourself, too, but you received nothing. You added another bolt; you drilled another hole; all day, a single operation, like a man allowed to eat but not to love, to feel but not to see, maimed and crippled, a whole life spent on something despised, performing with a single arm, one leg, a grunt. Using hours for a cheap currency, as if life were something stolen, counterfeit, to be gotten rid of at all costs. Long live the Factory, the State, the President, the Flag. Short live me.

[67]

Sid felt within himself a wild joy. Gently, with a lover's caress, he halted the wheel. The vase collapsed.

"Maybe your clay's too wet," advised Fat Stuff Halpern. "That's what kept happening to mine last summer, when I got interested in pottery. That's why I gave it up."

"Isn't it about time for you kids to get over to the rifle range?" said Sid, looking morosely at his clay pile. "I'm sure I heard the bugle," forgetting to encourage them to express.

"Don't get sore," said Norman. "Maybe we like it here more than shooting."

"Especially if the Lieutenant's mad at you for lying about that missing bullet," said Mel, winking.

Mike laughed. "That vase was lopsided, anyway," he said. "You're lucky it fell apart."

"On the double, fellas," barked Tannenbaum. "Get out of here."

Cohen was there ahead of them. "F' Christ's sake, Lieutenant," he said. "Why didn't you tell us you had another date? The rumor's all over camp you made out with the Big Chief's wife."

Flinn's mind worked feverishly. "I don't like to advertise, see."

"So that's why you were so keen on breaking away last night. We didn't have any idea. Usually the old girl waits till later in the season."

"The early bird gets my worm," chuckled the Lieutenant.

Cohen grinned. Once you got to know him, Flinn was all right. "I hear she's been making passes at that Tannenbaum guy."

"How's he made out?"

"Two balls, no strikes. He got his bat out there, but he ain't swinging."

"He's a jerk," said Flinn. "But I got to admit, Sylvia's no pushover."

Cohen smirked. "I hear she's been knocked for a homer just about every year since Omongo was erected."

He'd been tricked! He thought he was the hero, but he was just one more of her long string. With all her protests, her scratching, her biting, her pleading, it was she who'd won.

The Intermediates appeared, laughing and joking. Flinn snapped them to attention. "Men, instead of shooting at paper targets today, we're going to do something different: a sham battle, just like the Marines." First he showed them how to hug the ground with machine-gun bullets overhead. Then he showed them how to crawl up on the enemy, how to advance under fire.

They spread into the woods, shooting it out, charging, closing in; cutting up Fairy Godmothers; stabbing little Princesses; one by one, plunging their knives into Mother Goose; picking the eyes out of Snow White; strangling Red Riding Hood with her kerchief; whipping little Hansel with leather scourges; holding Gretel in the pot of boiling oil; ripping fingernails from anonymous elves; tearing wings out of picturebook fairies; chasing them, fleeing, screaming into the big stone castle high in the sky; swarming across the moat; leading their troops onward, battering down the gates; advancing, with banners, swords, axes, bayonets, plundering, killing, burning, looting . . .

Randy ran down the narrow pass between the huge boulders.

"There's one," they shouted. "An Arab, a sniper. Watch out, he's got hand grenades."

Randy ducked. Maybe the bushes would hide him. If only he'd stop breathing so hard. He put his hands over his mouth. It made it seem louder, like the snarling of a trapped tiger.

"Where'd that damned Arab go?"

"Just let me see him and I'll shoot his head right offa his shoulders." It was Mel, his own roommate. It sounded like another voice, someone who'd gone haywire.

"Hey, guys, look what Mel's got. A real bullet."

"How'd you get it?"

That's who! Norman hadn't lied. Mel stole it while Norm wasn't looking.

"You better throw it away. Flinn'll kill you if he finds out."

Randy peered over the boulder. Mel was showing off the bullet. He heard the bolt open, then close. If he ran now, they'd see him for sure.

Norm was up on the ledge, his rifle dangling. Sitting there, not even giving a darn, when his best friend, Randy, was trapped.

A machine gun. He'd give anything for one. He'd mow them down like ducks at a shooting gallery. Only these ducks would squawk with pain, squirting their blood like ketchup. He squeezed. BRRRRR. He wouldn't let go. BRRRRR.

The notes of the distant bugle trilled a sharp command. Like toy soldiers, they stopped in their tracks, their springs suddenly run down. They hesitated for a second, each in a different position, waiting to be wound, holding their tin rifles in the air.

Steiner lifted the needle. All over camp, in fields, canoes, on rafts, the little toy soldiers stopped what they were doing. Carefully, he placed a new record on the turntable; the loudspeaker blared its fake bugling; the little toys, rewound, revived, began to move again, singly, in groups, marching to different fields, toward new battles, exchanging bats for paddles, gloves for rifles, rifles for lumps of clay.

A SECRET BASTION

RANDY WALKED ALONE through the woods. He came to a narrow strip of water. An island, an island he'd never heard about. He dragged a log over and let it fall. He crawled across on his hands and knees. He put his foot down with a hard stamp to let everyone know it was his. His own secret island!

He sat down on a rock. This was like the bay back home, where no one could touch him. Just the place to work on his picture. He unrolled the piece of shelf paper.

A huge island almost filled the long paper. Harbors, cities, beaches, and in the center, a range of mountains. On the slopes, people were skiing, their mufflers trailing in the wind. One skier had fallen; a first-aid sled was rushing up the mountainside. The others were skiing past the man who was down, having too much fun to stop.

Where the mountains leveled off, there was a frozen pond. Dozens of ice skaters were gliding all over it, laughing and yodeling. Along the snow-packed shore, a bunch of swans huddled together for warmth, not knowing where to go since winter was here and the icy pond had filled with noisy people.

A giant circus tent. Three rings. A lion was attacking the trainer. He had a chair and a gun, too, just in case. In the center ring was a tightrope walker, way up, a hundred feet above the tiny faces of the crowd. He would fall any

[71]

second. A man talking into a microphone pointed up: "Don't be afraid, folks, we pay him a hundred dollars a night."

Some elephants were doing a dance in the third ring, their feet up in the air, about to stamp on the ground. The trainer had fallen. He was lying on the dirt, right under the raised-up foot of the biggest elephant. "Help, Help!" read the words. But everyone was looking at the tightrope walker, who was about to fall.

Randy drew a sunny beach filled with palm trees. A man had just been hit by a huge coconut. "Who hit me?" he was yelling. On the sand, in front of him, people were lying in the sun. Some people were swimming. One man was way out beyond the breakers. Coming toward him was a whole bunch of hungry sharks, their huge, teeth-filled mouths wide open, ready to rip him to bits . . .

Randy put away the scroll. Pieces of fireworks were floating on the water like toy sailboats. The water was dirty, like back home at the bay. He felt homesick.

How could he tell them he didn't like it at camp, that he didn't give a darn for the scholarship or for Steiner or for any of it? Why had they picked him to come, anyway? He was lousy at baseball, and no good at tennis or shooting. Just because his pop worked for Mike Oronsky's dad. There was something phony about the whole thing.

Some baby frogs with tails swam along the shore. Suddenly, a long black fish swallowed one, then darted away. He felt sick. He could feel the baby frog in the fish's throat, alive, still breathing, screaming, like his pet turtle in the sewer pipe. He felt as if *he* had swallowed the frog, the turtle. He wanted to cough up, but something kept them down, whole, unchewed, squirming around in his throat. Something terrible inside him kept forcing them back, where he could feel them scratching, crying, trying to get out.

Faintly, he heard the yells, the playful screams from the boathouse. What was he doing here! Their voices cut across the lake like a giant knife. Go back. He had to. He raced as fast as he could, faster, faster, past the tangled brush, over the bridge, through the woods. Suddenly he fell: the lion leaped; the tightrope snapped; the sharks came in for the kill.

MAIL CALL

Darling Randy,

Your Aunt Rose and Uncle Natie were here last night for a visit and guess who we talked about. It was you, darling. Aunt Rose said what a lucky boy it was who should have the honor to be sent to such a high-class Jewish camp. And Uncle Natie said he wishes someone sent him to a nice camp because he would make so many connections and gotten somewhere when he was grown up.

Darling. We are all frankly worried about the food up there. How is it? Tell me the truth. I'm your mother and you can tell me. I mentioned to your aunt that it was not kosher and she was truly disturbed. But then I told her she's foolish because that's the new style. This isn't Europe any more and besides Omongo is a million miles away in the woods where no one knows the difference if you eat a little bacon on the side because it's so far from everything even God can't find it. This makes her laugh.

How is the food? Do they give you juice every morning? Do they squeeze it from fresh oranges or do they give you that cheap canned stuff which I hear on the radio doesn't have any vitamins? How many times a day do they give you meat? Tell me so I can drop a note to Mr. Steiner and complain in case anything is wrong. Just because we're not paying doesn't mean I can't complain you know. My darling's health comes first, primarily, before anything else.

Uncle Natie and your father are looking at a wrestling fight on TV. Do you get eggs for breakfast every day? If you don't I want you to go to Mr. Steiner and insist. Immediate. If you don't speak up you'll never get anywhere in this world. Your Uncle Natie is laughing because the big man with the blond hair is being hit in the stomach by the other man's head. Your Uncle Natie tells me the dark one is Jewish and one of the best wrestlers on TV. Your father is telling me to put out the desk light but I will not because I love you too much and it is too important that I write to you and tell you not to forget to brush your teeth after every meal. You know what happened to your cousin Seymour. Don't forget to eat a good diet and make friends because later on in life what counts is the right friends. Look at your father god bless him who knows no one. We want you to grow up to be someone and get plenty of sun on your body. A growing boy needs vitamins which only the sun has. Don't forget to write please write me because it is very lonely here without you. There is nothing to do except drink cold seltzer and watch TV.

Your Aunt Rose has just come from the kitchen. She says the snacks are all ready and to tell you please do not drink coffee or it will make you even smaller than you are. I am hungry now and your father keeps telling me to put out the light so he can watch TV. You should see how terrible this Blond Bomber is. An Irishman I think. He is kicking our man in the chest with his foot. The judge looks like an anti-Semite and is doing nothing. No! The black-haired one is up and he has the Blond Bomber on the floor. We are all cheering for him and your father is telling me

*once more put out the light and the potato chips are here
and the coffee which I don't want you to take and get
plenty of sun.*

Love XXXXXX
Mama

Randy folded the letter carefully and stuffed it in his
pocket. He got out his pen and his writing pad.

Dear Mom and Pop, he wrote.

Something happened today that—Randy crossed it out
and began again. *Today we had arts and crafts and our
conselor Sid let me draw because I didn't like using clay.
It was real fun. After that we had swimming and you know
how I like that! Our conselor Sid is real nice but he's
usually not here at nights because he's busy at the arts and
crafts place making things. Tomorrow he says me and Norm
can go there and maybe I'll take him up on that. Especially
because from now on we won't be having arts and crafts
but baseball instead. It's because of a fight.* He crossed out
the last sentence. He started again.

"I don't go for Chevrolets," said Mike. "They're plain
tinny."

"You're crazy," said Mel. "The Chevrolet we have is
still good after two years."

"Two years!" cried Mike. "Must be some wreck. We
trade ours in every season."

"The Chevy's a cheap crate, same as a Ford," said Fat
Stuff.

"What kind of car you got, wise-guy, a Volkswagen?"

"A Chrysler Imperial Convertible," said Fat Stuff,
beaming.

"Phew," whistled Mel. "I got to admit those babies are
O.K."

"What year?" asked Mike.

"This year's, of course," said Fat Stuff. "My old man wouldn't be caught dead in an old car."

"That Chrysler's too damn conservative," said Mike. "My pop likes flash."

"It's got flash all right, inside, in the motor," said Fat Stuff, smugly. "We don't like things too showy."

"Hey, bright boy," shouted Mike across the tent. "What kind of car have you got?"

Randy looked up. "It's too much trouble keeping a car in the city," he explained.

"Too much trouble, hell!" said Mike. "You mean it's too expensive. Your dad don't even have enough to buy a jalopy."

"Why don't you ask what kind of car I've got?"

It was Greenberg. They stared at him as if he were displaying a special magic power.

"We saw it," said Mike, grudgingly. "My old man could afford a chauffeur too, only he ain't the type to show his money to every Tom, Dick and Harry."

"You jerks talk as if *you* owned the cars," shouted Norman. "You're not even old enough to drive. So Randy don't have a car. Neither do you." He went back to his sex book.

"Stooge," whispered Mel.

"His parents aren't even married," muttered Fat Stuff.

"Listen," said Mike, "my old man's promised me a brand-new car when I graduate high school."

"Where you going, Mike, out of town?" asked Mel.

"You don't think I'd go to a school in New York, do you? That's for cheapskates."

"I wouldn't go to one of those free city schools if they paid me," said Fat Stuff. "People'd ask me where I went and what would I say? Brooklyn College?"

"That's where the looey teaches," said Mel. "At Brooklyn."

[76]

"That's because he couldn't get a better job," said Fat Stuff.

"It's hard to get into an out-of-town school," said Mel. "Those out-of-town colleges all got Jewish quotas."

"Especially if you're from New York," said Mike. "That's why I'm glad we live in Great Neck."

"I'm already in," said Fat Stuff, carefully unwrapping a bar of Milky Way. "Ivy League." He sunk his teeth into the rich, creamy chocolate.

"How could you be accepted when you just started high school?" said Mel.

"What college?" challenged Mike.

His teeth went up and down like an overworked guillotine. "Can't say," he muttered. "Not allowed to. Only I can tell you this, it's one of the classiest schools in the East. My dad gave a whole pile of mazuma to their Alumni Fund."

"I don't believe it," said Mike. "Not an Ivy League school. No siree. Them schools got principles."

"Are you going to say you're Jewish when they ask you on the application?" asked Mel.

"I'm going to put down 'Hebrew,'" said Fat Stuff. "A lot of guys don't get in just because they're stupid enough to write down 'Jewish.'"

"You're right there," said Mike. "'Hebrew' looks a helluva lot better than plain old 'Jewish.'"

"I wonder what would happen," said Mel, "if you put down 'Atheist.'"

"You kidding!" said Fat Stuff, unwrapping a second bar. "No school would take you. You got to be something."

"Suppose you really don't believe in God?" said Mel.

"So what?" said Mike. "Nobody believes in God. But you still gotta have a religion."

Fat Stuff drew his feet up onto the blanket and rested his greasy head against the pillow.

[77]

"Where the heck do you get all that candy?"

"It's like getting into the right school," said Fat Stuff. "It takes pull."

"Yeah, how do you smuggle that junk in?" asked Mel.

"You make it sound like I'm taking dope," said Fat Stuff.

"Hey, bright boy," cried Mel. "What are you doing?"

"Levine's writing to his ma and pa," said Mike. "Telling 'em how he's never had it so good and how for a change he gets three square meals a day and a real roof over his head. He's telling 'em how he hates the idea of having to go back to that cold-water flat of theirs."

"You ever get a good look at that beat-up trunk of his?" said Mel.

The lake is terrific.

"Looks like it's made from an old crate," said Fat Stuff.

I keep dropping the ball.

"Looks like his old man brought it over from the other side," said Mike.

Maybe I can improve.

"You mean his old man's a foreigner!" cried Fat Stuff.

"He's just a cheapskate needle-stitcher for my dad," said Oronsky.

"You mean like a woman?" cried Mel. "He sews like a woman?"

"Tent Thirty-eight, stand by your sacks!" Cohen sprang up the steps. "Get this," he shouted. "I'm your new counselor. From now on, I'm the boss."

Randy took his letter and began to tear it up.

"Hey, buster, what's that?"

"Just a letter. I decided not to send it."

"We got no secrets here, Levine. Gimme."

"No," cried Randy, "please."

Cohen grabbed it. " 'Swimming is my . . .' " He joined

the scraps together. " '. . . is my favorite sport.' Now, isn't that nice. Swimming is his favorite sport."

"It's mine too, Daddy," said Mike.

"Me too," said Mel.

" 'The lake is really terrific.' "

"It's tho pwetty you could eat it," mocked Mel.

"Let's get down to the sexy part," said Mike.

"There isn't any," cried Randy.

" 'Only I don't like . . .' Wait a minute. 'Baseball.' Aw."

"The thewing-needle boy don't like batheball," said Mike. "I got something to add to that. Us baseball players don't like him!"

"Give it back!"

" 'The trees and scenery here are great.' "

"That's why he's so lousy in the outfield. Too busy admiring the view."

" 'The activities really keep me busy.' "

"Ain't that nice, Mama Levine?" said Mike.

"It sure is, Daddy Levine," said Mel, lifting an imaginary skirt to curtsy.

"I'm glad we sent him there, Mama Levine, with all them nice rich boys."

"We didn't send him, Papa. Don't forget. He was chosen. Our Randy baby is one of the chosen few."

"You mean the scholarship? That's 'cause he's such a good ball player, Mamala. Or is it for some other reason?"

" 'I hate it,' " shouted Cohen. " 'I want to go home. Send me a ticket. Why did you ever make me come? I can't . . .' "

"Go on," said Mike.

"That's all there is," cried Cohen. "That's when I came in." He grabbed hold of Randy. "Don't ever let me see you doing this again, Levine. That kind of filth is a reflection on me. From now on I'm gonna read every one of your letters."

MOPPING-UP OPERATION

▐▊▌▌▐▊▌▌▐▊▌▌▐▊▌▌▐▊▌▌▐▊▌▌▐▊▌

"WHAT ARE YOU ALL STANDING AROUND FOR?" shouted Cohen. "You heard what the man said. Lights out. Greenberg, put that book away. Let's see some action. Get out your flashlights."

"What's up?"

"Oronsky, grab a pail of water and start mopping. Greenberg, straighten out the trunks. Kahn, go outside and pick up every piece of paper you can find. I don't want to find a single scrap or it'll be your ass. I want this cabin spotless. Tomorrow morning when they hold the inspection, Tent Thirty-eight is going to get one hundred or my name ain't Cohen."

"They didn't say anything about an inspection tomorrow morning," said Mel.

"It's supposed to be a surprise. And I'll tell you a little secret: one of the main reasons they're having it is to see if there's any improvement in Tent Thirty-eight."

Mike and Mel nodded their heads glumly.

"It's not all your fault, it was Tannenbaum, too. But now things are different."

The campers in Tent 38 prepared for the surprise attack—the inspection at daybreak. Cohen shouted orders like a string of bullets. He showed them how to draw the blankets so tight they looked like drum skins. He made them search for dust on every post and beam, places they'd never

[80]

thought about. He even made them scrape between the floor boards. They were soldiers, their lives depending on it, sweeping a field for mines.

Finally he told them to sleep on the floors, because he didn't want to get their beds mussed up.

They clicked off their flashlights. The night enveloped them in its cold, dark shroud.

Randy looked at Norman, lying next to him, in the center of the floor. "You freezing, too?" he whispered.

"Yeah, damn it," said Norm. "All I got's one blanket."

"Same here," said Randy. He was shivering. "How about sleeping together?" he whispered. "It'd be warmer that way."

"O.K. with me," said Norman. They joined blankets. They huddled under the double wool thickness. He could feel the warmth from Norm's naked body. He felt better now, no longer alone. They were a team, merged beneath the blankets, fighting together, against Cohen, Steiner, the camp, the cold, oppressive air.

SNEAK ATTACK

THE BLACK SKY OPENED. Plants cupped their leaves upward, as if to catch the red drops. An old man rubbed his eyes, yawned, got up to go to work, and remembered: it was the first day of his retirement. He sat at the edge of the bed and wondered what to do. A salesman nervously dusted his sample case. The big one, the chain account, now or never. His hands shook. One more shot, a quicky, down the hatch. The sun rose higher. The leaves turned. A speculator rechecked his bids. His heart, hot cash, angina pectoris, the hot tip, the pain, the killing. A soldier looked through his sights. The cupped leaves broadened. The sky's slash widened. The prisoner crouched. The firing squad aimed. Ten bullets flashed through the red-hot air. A leaf dropped. A crow screamed. The old man fell to the floor. The salesman cringed. The tipster cried out in pain. Steiner looked at his chronometer.

The inspection. Four more minutes. He looked through the window at the forest, a dark cadaver sprawled alongside the camp.

Another year in the red. He felt like a surgeon, desperately hacking at the limbs in order to save the body, cutting away at food bills, repair bills. If only he could get at its heart. The fee. Economies could be sneaked in gradually, without anyone knowing it. But upping the fee would be fighting in the open, without a bush to hide behind. He needed help. He almost wanted to shout it: *Help!*

What about the Greenberg woman? Miracles did happen. And it wasn't really a miracle he wanted, just common decency. He stepped to the mirror. The poisonous morning light hit the silver in his graying hair. Morning? It was a time for mourning, for varicose veins, for hardening of the arteries. How lucky those campers, those counselors, no worries, just follow the schedule, winning stripes, medals, cups, their lives confined to the bare essentials: to hit the ball, to hit the target, to hit him with your right, your left, to win.

His own life was a succession of demands: higher pay for the waiters, more money for food, the parents' complaints, the endless creditors' phone calls, taxes, the winter repair bills, insurance premiums. It was easier just to take orders.

He checked his chronometer. He put the record on the turntable. This was it, the surprise inspection.

THE GREAT SPORT

"BATTER UP!"

The Iroquois are a single game ahead. The Sioux are out to even it up. Feinstein fishes for a wild one; a strike-out. Kaufman hits a line drive—safe on first. Greenberg, their lousiest, stands there like a target. Strike, strike, strike, a machine gun. Levine steps up, clumsy, ready to swing with all his might. Strike one.

Randy prays, careful, keep your eyes on the ball, don't be fooled. A good one may look bad; a bad one may look good. Strike two. Oronsky is hopping mad. Strike three.

Tricked! What was bad had looked good. Randy wants to take the bat and kill himself, a sacrifice for the team. Dead, a hero. Randy Levine, hoooraay! They take possession of the field.

The sun burns. Grasshoppers screeching sharp, violent songs jerk about like dried-up skeletons. If only they'd switch him to another team, the Juniors. Steiner would never allow it. Randy would break an arm. That'd be enough to keep him out for the whole season.

Randy chases the hard white, dirty white, goddam ball. Into the woods. A yellow butterfly. Follow it. Escape.

Branches snap against his bare legs like brown whips. A pointed twig rips his shirt. The forest floor is dark as the subway, darker even than the sunless shaftway in front of his bedroom. A hiding place for the night.

"What are you crawling around here for!" Randy looks up. It's Eagle, his eyes so far back you can only see the hollows staring like pieces of black glass. The skin on his face is pulled so tight his head looks like a skull. "Spyin' on me, ain't you!"

"I just came to get the ball," whispers Randy.

Eagle is making a lean-to out of branches. "Want to buy some candy bars? That why you came?" He chooses them carefully, walking like an animal, a cat.

"What you building?" asks Randy.

"It's for the Omongo."

"You mean for us? I mean them, the guys?"

"The Omongo tribe. Way back there, boy, in the woods. Every year the tribe gets bigger and braver, and all the time you people thinks the Omongos are dead and you go on cutting down their trees and running around their woods, and the Omongos get madder and cry out for their land. It belongs to them, not you! Go back with them Jew campers where you belong."

Randy runs back to the abandoned field. Angrily, he picks up a stone. With all his might, he throws it, fast, like a bullet cutting through the sky, past second, past the mound, straight to home base, in a long, clean, perfect swoop. It's his first good throw.

SKIRMISH

▮▮▮▮▮▮▮▮▮▮▮▮▮▮▮▮▮▮▮▮▮▮▮▮▮▮▮▮▮

STEINER BENT OVER HIS REVISED SCHEDULE, admiring the hard thinking that had filled the hundreds of squares with added competitions, with new rivalry, with steak once a week instead of twice. He gazed at it as if it were a masterpiece.

"What are you doing?"

He jumped. "Sylvia, stop crawling down those stairs like a cat."

"A cat?" she meowed. "Why don't you buy me a bell." She laughed. "Only who will tie it on?"

"You've got a ghoulish sense of humor. Too bad no one's recognized your true talent."

"I don't like sarcasm, Harry."

"I don't, either. Especially when it comes to Omongo. It doesn't take a bookkeeper to know you can't keep subtracting from something you don't have. Minus, minus, minus. You go behind my back, and spend all the money I manage to earn."

"Necessary expenses," she said coolly. "I spend money for the same reason you play General, ordering your little eight-year-old troops around."

"It satisfies my creative urge," he mocked. "Sort of like painting."

"Only I get reviews," she said. "Raves."

"Just a little bribe, that's all it takes."

"Bribe?" She picked the word out of the gutter with

the dirt still clinging. "Renting a gallery isn't like bribing the State Health Commission, Harry. But I can't expect you to know anything about art."

"I know how it smells," he said. "How you stand the odor of turpentine in that bedroom is beyond me."

"Oh, is that the reason you're never there?"

"Forget it," her bullets piercing his armor. "How's your painting coming?"

"What I need is time," she sighed. "I know I have the talent. I'm ahead of them."

"Why don't you stop painting for a year? Maybe they'll catch up."

"Stop joking," Sylvia snapped. "Art isn't that simple. You have to know the right critics. You've got to know what style they're looking for."

"Listen, twenty-five years ago, when I bought Omongo . . ."

"Bought! Please, Harry. You mean stole. From a half-breed moron."

"First you tell me I'm too thick. Now you say I'm shrewd. Which is it?"

"Both. You were shrewd at first. But now you're possessed by your little kingdom. Every summer you leave that hack teaching job and put on your royal robes. King Harry, King of the Omongos. And his wife, Queen Sylvia." She curtsied.

"Cut it out." His voice was weary. "You know why I'm not principal just as well as I do. I refuse to compromise," he smiled at his pun, "my principles."

"What principles, Your Majesty, pray tell?"

"When I first bought this place—yes, no matter what you say, I have the bill of sale—it was nothing but a desolate wilderness, nothing but trees. Little by little, I cleared the land, I . . ."

As if he'd fought off those blood-thirsty Indians himself, she thought. She could see him in his purple vestments, with that savage, last-of-the-Omongos handyman, Paul Eagle, chopping down the big red cherry tree. Harry Steiner, the coon-hatted Jew, sputtering away how money could never concern him as much as character, how Omongo was a training grounds for the young, training them to fight their way through the bitter years.

She looked into his face as if examining the crude strokes, the shoddy draftsmanship, the careless choice of pigments. "Harry, stop playing the Great White Father. You're not great; you're a little man. You're not white; your heart's as black as slime. I know where you go with that station wagon, night after night. To every town slut you can buy. And you're no father; you never will be. Little, black and sterile, that's what you are. Great White Father—it's a lie! A great white lie!"

"Stop shouting, Sylvia. I've got plans."

"What, to sell out to some garment manufacturer?"

"That Greenberg woman. She's rich as an oil field, Sylvia. I charged her a higher rate for her son and she didn't even know it. 'Send the bill,' she said. And even if she knew, she wouldn't have cared."

"Just because she's willing to send her son here doesn't mean she's willing to support the whole damned camp." Sylvia walked toward the door. "I've heard too many of your wild ideas. I believe in hard realities." She smiled lewdly.

For the first time, he noticed the green toreadors, the skin-tight sweater. "For a boys' camp, Sylvia, isn't that a bit extreme? If I were you, I'd dress a little plainer."

"But you're not me, Harry. You forget."

He looked at her anxiously. "But I don't forget who *you* are. And don't you forget it either. You're my wife."

"How does that change anything?"

Before he could think of an answer, she left.

[87]

One of the windows in the arts and crafts shack was stuffed with aging newspapers. Weeds all over the place. He could have had Paul clean up. But no, the arts were expendable. It was his way of hating her.

She could see Sid Tannenbaum's face through the dirty windowpane. She'd say she'd left some paint tubes around. It would give them something to talk about. Wasn't he an artist, too?

A camper. She recognized him, the Greenberg boy, working on a large clay cup. The one whose mother would save Omongo, St. Greenberg of Arc. So, the fate of the camp rested on his mother's shoulders. Or was it her breasts? If saving Omongo depended on Harry's amorous talents, the camp was done for. She opened the door and entered without knocking.

ARTS AND CRAFTS

NORMAN RIPPED OFF a piece of clay. It was right; it resisted. Good clay fought back.

Sid looked worried. "Where's your friend?"

"Randy says he's going to learn baseball if it kills him. That's all him and Mike talked about at supper. Mike's teaching him how to bat."

"Good grief," moaned Sid. "He'll never finish his scroll now that Steiner's canceled Intermediate arts and crafts."

"I told him he could come," said Norman. "But he was

so busy talking about the best grip that the jerk didn't even hear me."

"Honestly, it's enough to get you sick," complained Sid. "Here I'm trying to bring out the best in you fellas, and all Randy cares about is baseball."

Norm shrugged. If only Tannenbaum would knock it off so they could have some quiet. He smoothed the sides of the big loving cup.

Tannenbaum stared morosely out the window. He felt as if he'd lost a son. "Randy will end up being just one more cog in an assembly-line conveyer belt," he warned. "Running on paychecks instead of electricity. He'll never know the joy of being creative."

"So forget him," muttered Norman, adding a coil of clay.

"Last summer I had a job on a conveyer," said Sid. "It was like a bed of spikes. But for the others, it was filled with pennies, a river to be panned for gold. All that mattered was the money. Live it up on the weekends. The other five days didn't exist." He looked sad.

"Shit!" said Norman, starting all over again. "This gotta be perfect," trying to shut out Sid's voice.

Sylvia Steiner entered without knocking. "I left some tubes of paint here last season," she said, her voice too brisk, too nervous. "I was hoping they might still be around. Incidentally, dear," she turned on Norman sweetly, "wasn't that the bugle I heard?"

"Damn it," said Norman, putting away the cup. "I'll be late." She closed the door after him.

"I'm awfully sorry about what happened, Sid." She sat down beside him on the bench.

"I suppose your husband's been complaining about me," he said sullenly.

"I never talk shop with him. But I heard he switched you from the thirteen-year-olds to the Midgets. I want you to know Harry's decisions have nothing to do with me. The fact that our tag names are the same, as the saying goes, is purely coincidental."

"You mean you just happen to be coincidentally married."

"He talked me into it," she smiled. "Just the way he must have fooled you into coming here."

"Guess I was fooled, all right," giving the wheel an angry kick. "I thought I'd have a chance to be expressive here. But creativity gets in the way of guys like Steiner."

She leaned forward with a bright smile. He felt inspired. "The only property a man ever really owns is his life," he said, earnestly. "Everything else is just on loan: books, houses, summer camps. Sooner or later it all gets put up on the auction block, and what we thought was ours really didn't belong to us at all. It was just something to use for a little while."

"So everything's up for sale, is it?" she mocked, adjusting a glistening earring. "How can I find out the price?" What a handsome, innocent child!

"All we have is our own life. We can throw it down the drain or devote it to a cause. But we should have the right to do whatever we want with it!"

"Isn't that rather hedonistic?" she asked, slyly.

"Most people give in," he said, remembering his term paper in philosophy. "They salute the bright colors and learn to kill for the sake of another name on a map. They pile corpses to the glory of Uncle Sam or John Bull or the Russian Bear."

Sylvia was concerned. Maybe he was a leftist. But a gorgeous one—that made all the difference in the world. "Sid," she put her hand on his shoulder. "I'm glad my husband hired you. I really am."

"So am I," he affirmed. "I want to teach these kids how to discover themselves. It's a hard, dangerous voyage, and once they start, it may be too late to turn back. But maybe the only way to get along in a world that's gone off its rocker is to forget the slogans and the battle cries, and live our own lives in our own way, secretly, if we have to, in our own little studios, at our own little workbenches."

A bad childhood, she thought. Probably neurotic. But then, who wasn't, these days? "Don't you believe in compromise just a little?" she asked softly, wishing she could be the one to compromise him.

"Never!" he vowed, his voice rising with emotion. "That's what parents and schools and camps want, to make us compromise. That's what Omongo wants. To kill all the good in people." His fingers twitched, as if he were shaping a clay masterpiece.

She crushed her cigarette in a weird blue-green ashtray. "And is there any room in this terrible world of yours . . ." She put her hand on his knee. ". . . any room for love?"

Sid turned red. "Maybe making a better vase is my way of making love."

A long, embarrassed silence. "What a curious ashtray," she said, examining it. "Something you made, Sid?"

"Yeah, it's a new glaze." He looked interested again.

"Beautiful," she said, looking into his eyes. Slowly, with exaggerated care, to display her interest in preserving the arts, she laid the ashtray down. "Sid, I think you have what it takes to be an artist. I think people will go for your things in a big way." Such strong, masculine hands.

"I don't want to care who goes for them."

"Don't you have any ambitions?"

"I want to be indifferent to words like ambition and success. I don't want anything more than steady fingers, and time enough to make my next vase."

Filled with young, foolish ideas. So adolescent. But well developed. She hadn't had anyone like him in a long time. "I can help you," she said, taking his hand in hers.

"We could open a crafts shop together. Provincetown. Greenwich Village."

Taps rang out. He began making the final rounds, clicking off lights, closing drawers. "I have to go now. I'm supposed to put the kids to bed."

"Kids." She smiled to herself. "How about it?" she asked. "I've got plenty of capital."

Hurriedly, Sid snapped out the last light. The moon silhouetted his tall, young body. "It's kind of late," he said nervously.

"Think it over," she said, putting her hand on his cheek.

"Thanks a lot, Mrs. Steiner," he blurted. "It sounds like a wonderful opportunity." He gave her a puzzled stare, then bolted out the door.

The room was empty.

NOSE-DIVE

"LINE UP!" shouted Fat Stuff Halpern, chewing away at his chocolate-coated, cream-centered candy bar.

"You eat any more, you'll drown," shouted Mike.

"I can float." Fat Stuff licked his lips.

"You're so filled with candy, you'll sink right to the bottom," warned Mel.

"You'll get cramps," said Mike.

"So I'll just take a crap."

"Hey, guys," screamed Mel. "Don't swim near Fat Stuff. He shits in the water."

"I'll bet he uses fish to wipe with," said Mike. "That's why you see all them dead perch floating around."

"Hell, he don't use plain old fish," said Mel. "He uses eels. Sticks 'em up his ass. That way he gets a nice big charge."

Cohen turned to the Intermediates. "The high board," he announced with a smile. It was so high it made them dizzy just to look up, soaring above them like a great bird with its wings outstretched. "I'm going to execute a few dives, to show you what can be done."

He stood at the rear of the platform, eyes straight ahead, arms at his sides, body erect. He began running to the edge of the board, then over, into space. Halfway out he coiled as if in pain, then twisted free, falling down, down . . .

Cohen emerged. Triumphantly he climbed onto the raft, not even acknowledging the "great's" and the "how'd you do it's?"

"Show-off," whispered Randy.

"Yeah, wouldn't you show off if you were that good?"

Randy kept quiet. He hadn't thought of it that way.

"Regular formation!" shouted Cohen. They shuffled into place like a pack of cards. The Kings were in back, certain the bugle would blow before they were called on. The Jokers, the short ones, were out in front, nervously waiting to be played. "Smart aleck!" said Cohen, pointing to Randy. "Greenberg's ahead of you."

"I don't mind being first," said Randy.

"Listen here, buster, I don't give a damn what you mind. Greenberg goes first."

"I only got ahead because they're all afraid," muttered Randy.

"Who's afraid?" shouted Cohen.

Slowly, a small hand raised itself from the deck. "I am," said Greenberg.

"You are what?"

"Scared shitless," said Norman. He didn't yell it. He didn't whisper it, either. Just in between, as if he were telling a dirty joke.

"Coward!" cried Cohen. "You've been afraid all season. Now are you going to learn the easy way, or do you want the special treatment?" Norman just stood there. Cohen dragged him up the ladder. "All right, wise-guy," his voice trembling with anger. "Let's see you dive."

Norm grabbed Cohen's arm. They fought for balance. Cohen's face was a giant cherry bomb about to explode.

Together they fell.

BIVOUAC

▮▮▮▮▮▮▮▮▮▮▮▮▮▮▮▮▮▮▮▮▮▮▮▮▮▮▮▮▮▮▮

"MAJORITY RULES!" yelled Flinn.

"This is a democracy!" shouted Cohen.

"Maybe it's gonna rain," whined Fat Stuff. "I'll settle for the Woodsman Medal. One day of camping's enough for me."

"Sissy!" yelled Mike. "I want the gold Trailblazer. Our parents are going to be up in a few days. We want something we can be proud of."

"Three days is too long," complained Randy.

"What right have you got to vote?" demanded Mike. "You didn't even pay."

"Let's get it over with," said Lieutenant Flinn.

"Secret ballot," insisted Randy.

"Secret, hell," said Cohen. "We take our vote out in the open, like men."

"Up with them golden hands," shouted Mike. "F' Christ's sake, let's have some team spirit and vote for the Trailblazer."

Mel raised his fingers. Fat Stuff gave in, too.

"Hell, I'm no sore loser," said Randy, finally holding up his arm. Unanimous, except for Greenberg.

They entered the forest, laughing, as if it weren't a medal they were after at all, but fun. "Me Chinee," said Fat Stuff, pulling his hands into his sleeves. "Me know how to screw Chinee woman who got one sideways."

"Ah's a nigger boy," said Mel. "Only thing is, ah scared of dis here jungle."

"Oim from the good ol' sod," said Mike. "Kiss me blarney stone."

"Kiss me fat ass," said Fat Stuff, bending.

"Sho 'nuff, man," said Mel, leaning toward Fat Stuff.

"Chinee no like nigger lips on yellow behind," screamed Halpern, jumping away. "Chinee like Irish lips."

Flinn smiled. "Here's the trail, you guys," as if he had pulled it out of a hat. Fallen trees lay like telephone poles, their wire branches twisting around the path, trying to strangle it. The sun disappeared behind the heavy foliage, as they fought their way through a patch of dagger-pointed briars. Then it found them again, a relentless prison searchlight doggedly trailing a band of escaping convicts.

"What is this," complained Norm, "a goddam race?"

Randy shrugged. Greenberg was sure a poor sport. This was even better than the Bronx Zoo. No bars, no KEEP OFF signs.

"Look," shouted Fat Stuff, "a chipmunk!"

"Maybe you could eat him," said Mel.

"Cheap, cheap," said Mike. "I'm a cheapmunk."

[95]

"Is not kosher," chanted Fat Stuff. "Cheap monk belong to wrong church."

"Kosher's a lot better," said Mel. "The other stuff's poisonous sometimes."

"It all comes from the same cow," said Norm. "It's just a racket to make more money for the Jewish butchers."

"You guys are making me hungry," said Fat Stuff. "Flinn even found the candy I hid in my poncho, the son-of-a-bitch."

"But you just ate breakfast."

Mike looked at Fat Stuff gravely. "What's a candy bar worth to you?"

Fat Stuff's eyes blazed. "You got something?"

"Chocolate," whispered Mike.

"How much?" cried Halpern in ecstasy. Mike pulled an inch of chocolate wrapped in toilet paper from his pocket. "Is that all?" groaned Fat Stuff.

"You don't want it, I'll eat it myself," threatened Mike, peeling off the paper. The chocolate glistened like a deep-colored jewel.

"I'll take, I'll take," whispered Fat Stuff, excitedly. "How about a dime?"

"You kidding?"

"Fifteen."

"A quarter, or I'll eat it myself."

"Twenty," shouted Fat Stuff, desperately, grabbing the chocolate and thrusting two dimes into Mike's outstretched hand. In a second it was gone.

"Old Fatso went for it like a hungry dog," Mike whispered to Mel. " 'America's Favorite,' " he grinned, reading the wrapper: " 'America's Favorite Chocolate Laxative for Konstipated Kiddies.' "

Cohen took charge of building the campfire. "That should burn all night," he announced, like an expert.

Fat Stuff moved toward the flames. "You know," he confessed, wiping his forehead, "I don't feel so hot."

"You ought to feel hot," said Mel. "You're hogging the whole fire."

"I'm going to the john," announced Fat Stuff.

"Ain't none. You have to go in the woods," said Mike, leering. "And f' Christ's sake, don't go where we have to smell it."

"Hey, Lieutenant, where's the toilet paper?" asked Fat Stuff.

"In my pack," said the Lieutenant. "Levine! You and Greenberg get your flashlights and help him clear a path."

"Hurry," cried Fat Stuff, "I can't hold it in much longer."

Four dim circles of light broke through the forest, following what looked like a trail. "Can't wait," groaned Fat Stuff.

"Go ahead," said Flinn. He stared at the others. "You guys have to go?" They shook their heads. "What are you, shy or something? Get that limb out of the way," he said angrily. He pointed his light from behind as they stooped to struggle with the fallen branches.

Randy spotted something. A tiny green snake. He stuffed it in his pocket, before Flinn could see.

"All right, you kids," said the Lieutenant. "Let's hit the sack." He directed his light along the path back to the bonfire.

Cohen picked a good smooth spot for his sleeping bag. "Make sure there's no animals," he said. "I don't want a rattler crawling in."

"Don't worry," said Flinn. "I've lived in the jungle. There's no rattlers around here." Cohen was glad he was with the looey. You could trust a guy that was older, more experienced.

Randy and Norm spread out their bags. "Wait till you

see what I got," whispered Randy. "A little surprise for that big hero, Cohen."

"Why start a fight?" said Norman. "It pays to mind your own business around this fucking place."

"After what he's been doing to you all summer in swimming, don't you want to get even?"

"Listen, Levine, you get even with Cohen, and then he'll have to get even with you again. It'll never end."

"He won't know who did it," said Randy, sneaking up on the counselors' tent like a thief with his little green revolver. He shot the snake through the narrow opening.

Fat Stuff came running down the path. The canvas rose like a giant whale coming up for air. "Help!" screamed Cohen. "Rattler!" Cohen leaped out and grabbed hold of Halpern. "Quick," he yelled. "Serum!"

Randy smothered his laughs in his blanket. "Some serum for the swimming champ," he announced. "Toss it from the high-diving board."

"Let go!" yelped Fat Stuff. "I gotta go." Cohen held on.

"What in hell's the trouble?" shouted Flinn.

"Crap!" shrieked Fat Stuff. "Too late!"

The Intermediates howled and hooted . . .

It was the morning of the second day. The sky hardened into a diseased, purple mask. The air was hot and humid, like inside a closed coffin. The path disappeared among the tombstone trees. A bolt of lightning; a shout of thunder. The mourners huddled together.

"We'll get lost," said Cohen. "Eagle must have given us the wrong directions. You can't trust an Indian," he added, remembering a movie he'd seen.

"Rain!" screamed Fat Stuff.

"Knock it off," yelled Lieutenant Flinn. "A little water won't hurt you."

They groaned as the rain hit the leaves like falling shrapnel. "Let's take a break," they begged.

"Sissies!" cried Flinn, thinking of the harshest possible punishment. "Keep out of the Marines! We don't want fags like you." They scuttled along the vast forest floor, a line of crabs following the King Crab, Flinn, through the watery wastes, over the mud. They couldn't see. The whole world was turning upside down, drowning.

Randy tripped. Damn it—his heel! He limped on, as if he'd lost not just a heel, but his whole leg. The water began soaking through. He could feel it crawling into his stockings. What if he got trench foot? What if they had to amputate? He'd have to use a crutch, he'd be a crummy little cripple, he wouldn't be able to get out of the house when his mother started pestering him.

The rain poured down his face as if he was crying. Crying about being here, in the woods, in Omongo, a place he hated.

"What do you want?" snapped Flinn.

"I can't walk. I lost my heel."

"You damn fool," shouted Cohen, the rain-tears pouring down his face as if he was crying harder than everybody else. "Get back in line where you belong. It's hard enough to find this path without you making trouble."

If only he were a regular camper, instead of on a lousy scholarship. The fee made the difference. He could disappear right now into the woods, and they'd never care. Long as they didn't have to make a refund. If only he could take off his wet clothes, dry himself with a white towel, get into a pair of clean, dry shorts his mother had just ironed, still hot, hugging his body, warming it.

Norm put his arm on Randy's shoulder. They trudged on through the rain.

It was the evening of the second day. Rain thrashed and thunder pounded. The campers huddled under black ponchos, masked intruders shielding themselves with their cloaks.

Cohen's spongy face was worried. "What if they tell?"

"It's our tent, isn't it?" demanded Flinn.

"But suppose they're mad about sleeping in the rain while we're inside?"

"When they get those medals, they'll forget all about it. I know guys who got filled with lead in the war. A Purple Heart or two, a Presidential Citation and, man, they were almost glad they got hit."

They crawled inside the tent. A leak had sprung in one of the corners. Flinn made sure to sleep on the other side, where it was dry. Poor Cohen, the chump. What a Jew-boy. "See you in the morning," smiled Flinn. "And stop worrying. If you slept out in the rain with them, the kids would lose their respect for you."

Cohen lay down. "Hey, Lieutenant, there's a hole here. I'm soaked."

"Call the plumber," groaned Flinn, turning over. "Only let me get some shut-eye." He flicked off the flashlight.

"Prick," muttered Cohen, feeling for something to plug up the hole.

"I'd give anything for a tent," cried Randy, trying to get closer to the tree, where it was a little drier.

Greenberg pushed back his wet hair. "At least you voted for it, jerk. Don't you think I'm as wet as you are?"

"When my mom comes up," said Randy, "I'm going to tell her all about how we had to sleep in the rain and the damn counselors had a nice warm tent."

"You won't tell a goddam thing," said Oronsky. "Don't forget, bright-boy, you can't complain about something you haven't even bought. It took a lot of string-pulling to get you that scholarship, Levine. Ever figure out why *you* won it, when a thousand other guys would have given their right arms for the chance?"

Randy shrugged stupidly. He didn't know what to say. The heck with him . . .

The dark morning of the third day. They trudged forward, through enemy fire, bullets of rain ricocheting from the rocks, bouncing off their ponchos, dripping through their hair.

"Cheer up!" cried Flinn.

"Hey, Looey, when are we going to eat?" cried Fat Stuff Halpern.

"We decided against it," said Flinn. "We'll wait till we get back to camp."

"We'll starve to death," cursed Halpern.

The tribe of penitents marched, soaked by puddles, whipped by branches. Fat Stuff groaned. His was a special pain. He didn't want to hear any more jokes about his appetite. He just wanted to be saved, to be back in camp, attacking a huge turkey dinner. First the soup, then the turkey and stuffing, then the cranberry sauce, then doubles in all four, then French fries and doubles in that, then a big French-dressing salad and chocolate ice cream topped with hot fudge, topped with whipped cream, topped with walnuts and pistachios, topped with a big juicy cherry. Then doubles in the whole thing.

Scholarship or no scholarship, Randy would spill the beans. Old Man Steiner would take down every word, while Randy squealed, blabbed, split the case wide open. "Cohen!" He'd shout it for everyone to hear. Cohen would be scared stiff, not knowing whether to try to lie or run away. But the Great White Father would think of an excuse. The parents would say he dreamed it. Randy's mother would slap him in front of everyone. Cohen would win again.

He'd have to get even some other way. Lure him to the secret island, knock him in the head with a stone, just hard enough to keep him down while he tied him with a rope, tight, so it'd cut. He'd start pulling out the hair, yanking it like a bunch of weeds. Cohen would beg for mercy. He'd pull out the eyelashes. The lids, too. But not the eyes. He wanted Cohen to see everything. He wanted to look at the terror in Cohen's eyes as he ripped off the shirt, grabbing the hair on Cohen's chest. Cohen would shriek for pity like a cackling turkey, while Randy, the crazy butcher, stripped off the feathers. He'd gouge holes in Cohen's jaws, deep enough to see the bloody teeth gnashing. He'd use the can opener and pry out the teeth. Cohen would scream and beg. You couldn't even understand because his gums were leaking all over. He'd stick a knife under Cohen's nails, and pry. One by one, they'd pop off. Then he'd bore a hole into Cohen's forehead, right down to the brain, the nerves wriggling and shaking. Cohen's toothless mouth would moan in agony. But Randy wouldn't say a word; he wouldn't tell him how he hated him. He'd just keep working, punching holes, rubbing in salt. One last thing. He had to do one more thing while Cohen could still see, while Cohen could still feel. He worked the blade across a sharp rock. Cohen's eyes would follow every move like a dumb animal. He'd flinch as Randy bent down, jerked at the bloody trousers, and stripped off the jock. Cohen would look on in horror as the knife gleamed in the sun. Then, with all his might, in a single slash, he'd hack it off, right at the roots, and plunge the slimy mess into Cohen's gaping mouth. Then he'd seal Cohen's lousy lips forever, sew them up, like his old man, with a needle and . . .

"We made it!" yelled Cohen in triumph.

"I told you," beamed Flinn. The rain streamed down his cheeks; his wet brown hair looked like a pasted wig. His face was the mask of a gentile Moses preaching in the wilderness, leading the Jews to their promised Omongo, the land of milk and medals.

"Let's have them Trailblazers," cried Mike.

"Pin it right here," said Fat Stuff, eagerly wiping the mud off his poncho.

"One at a time," said Flinn.

"What the hell!" screamed Mike. "It's the wrong medal."

"Shut up," roared Flinn. "It's the Trailblazer, isn't it?"

"But it's supposed to be gold."

"Lousy old silver!" said Mel.

"Cool off," shouted Flinn. "Silver's the top medal this year. Gold's too expensive."

"Balls!"

"You know what the Woodsmen got—a worthless felt stripe." Everyone laughed.

"So it ain't gold," said Randy. "It's better than nothing."

"C'mon, let's have 'em," demanded Fat Stuff.

Flinn handed out the pieces of silver. Norm looked at his. "I don't want your lousy fake medal," he said. They gasped, as if they'd been harboring a lunatic. "A hunk of tin can pasted to a lousy safety pin," shouted Norm. He threw it into the woods.

Flinn's fingers slashed across Greenberg's mouth. Cohen smiled.

FAMILY REUNION

STEINER STOOD at the gate like a butler. "Hello there," he cried, running up to the Chrysler convertible. "How are you?" he asked jauntily, trying to remember the name. He'd seen them before, many times. Who in God's name were they?

"Tired. What a trip," said the man. "Is land so cheap here, you can't be closer?"

"Not if you want scenery like this," beamed Steiner, pointing to a tree. "You don't have that near New York." He'd have to have it chopped. Too close to the road; some of its leaves were beginning to block out the Omongo letters on top of the gate. "Breathe that fresh air," said Steiner, stretching his arms. "You can't tell me you get air like this in the city."

"How is our Berney?" asked Mrs. Halpern.

"Just fine," said Steiner. "Wonderful chap," suddenly remembering that Intermediate, the one who used to wet the bed. "Wait till you see how he's filled out," he said, thinking of all the candy that Fat Stuff must have smuggled in from Eagle.

"We're dying to see him," said Mrs. Halpern.

"How's the shoe business?" asked the Great White Father.

"Lousy, plain old lousy," said Mr. Halpern, as they headed for the Social Hall.

Another car. Steiner brushed his thinning hair. If only he had a mirror. He put out his cigarette. It was better to be seen without one. Stern, disciplined, that was the way to look.

The voices from Tent 38 echoed across the lake. "So I says to him, 'Max,' I says, 'cut it out. I can't make it any cheaper.' 'Oronsky,' he says, 'you gotta. With business like it is, you could stand in Macy's front window at high noon, naked...'"

"Please," shouted Mrs. Oronsky, "the children!"

"He looks just like you," shouted Mrs. Kahn, examining Mike once more.

"Everyone says he looks so much more like my husband."

"He does look like your husband. But the eyes, Mrs.

[104]

Oronsky, they're yours. The chin and nose are his, but the eyes are yours."

"So Max is about to sign when . . ."

"Everyone else thinks Michael has my husband's eyes and my chin," said Mrs. Oronsky.

"They're wrong," said Mrs. Kahn.

Cohen walked up the stairs, his smile kindly, confident, smug. "Welcome, Mr. and Mrs. Oronsky," he bowed. "And Mr. and Mrs. Kahn. You have a nice trip?" He looked around. "Where are the other folks?"

"You mean the Greenbergs?" cried Mrs. Oronsky. Norman put down his book. "Oh," she said, too late, "I mean *Mrs.* Greenberg, of course." Her face reddened. How terrible. Divorce. In Mexico. A country without water even.

"She's coming by car," muttered Norman.

"How nice," beamed Mrs. Oronsky.

Norman lay back on his bed. Why didn't they lay off?

Cohen looked happy. His big chance for a good tip. Maybe he'd go over when no one was around, and tell Mrs. Greenberg, frankly, just how much he was teaching that little son of hers: how he'd taught him to swim, at least some; how he'd taught him discipline, to obey.

"They're coming by bus," said Randy. "My dad doesn't own a car." They looked at him through the bars, like visitors in a zoo.

"Don't he go for the new models?"

"Now, Michael," whispered Mrs. Oronsky. "Tolerance, please. It's no fun to be," she paused, "in straitened circumstances."

"Randy darling!" His mother jumped out of the Omongo station wagon.

"Mama," he cried.

"Baby, let me look at my baby." Mrs. Levine, perspiring in her summer muskrat, held him in her arms.

"How can Mama look when you keep hugging her like that," complained his father.

"Here." He opened his fist.

"A medal!" cried Mrs. Levine. "Jacob, our son, a medal winner."

"Let me touch," said Mr. Levine. He held it up to the light. " 'Trailblazer.' "

"It's the top prize."

"The top!" she exclaimed. "Our boy, the top!"

"Well, I'm not the only . . ."

"Please," she cried. "You're like your father. Always so modest." She kissed him. She hugged him. It was worth all that rain and mud.

"Is it real?"

"Sure, Mom," said Randy.

"Real silver!" She waved it in the air. "If that isn't something."

"I'll bet it's worth plenty," said Mr. Levine.

"Next year there'll be a gold one."

Mr. Levine turned. "What's he think I am," he whispered, "a genius? Oronsky's favors don't come easy."

She held the medal to her black dress. "What a broach this would make."

"Keep it."

"You're fooling."

"I want you to wear it, Mom. It's yours."

"Darling." She was crying. "This is the proudest . . ." Mrs. Levine reached for her handkerchief. " . . . highpoint in my whole life." The tears streamed down her face. "I'll wear it every day. No matter what color dress." She ran her fingers through his hair.

"Esther, please, they're all looking. No demonstrations."

"Let 'em look," she shouted. "Jacob darling, I'm the happiest woman in the whole world." She pinned the medal to her dress like a pledge pin.

They walked up the cabin steps, the three of them. The door was too narrow. Jacob let go, trailing behind, like a sullen bridesmaid.

Cohen was a different person, smiling, laughing. Randy stopped, as if they'd entered the wrong cabin.

"My best friend, Norm Greenberg," said Randy.

"How do you do," beamed Mrs. Levine, trying not to look awed. She'd heard from Jacob, who'd heard from Mr. Oronsky, that the Greenbergs were rich as gold. Leave it to Randy. A wonderful thing, friendship. She should only have friends like that. "Norman darling, where's your parents? I'd like very much to meet them." She looked at Randy's foot pressing on her new shoes.

"They're getting a divorce," said Norman.

"Oh!" she exclaimed. Maybe she was wrong. Maybe he wasn't from such a fine family after all. How could you even call them a family? At least she and Jacob were together. Maybe they weren't so rich, but at least they were married.

"Who are your other friends?" she whispered, steering them toward the Oronskys, away from Norman.

"Hello, Mr. Oronsky." They stared at her. "Hello, Mrs. Oronsky. A pleasure it is to see you looking so well. Did you have a nice trip? Jacob tells me you got a new car. Congratulations. Best of luck." Before they could answer, she turned to the others.

"Mr. and Mrs. Kahn. I believe we met at the railroad station. And this must be your son, Melvin. He looks like Mr. Kahn." She examined the merchandise more closely. "And the hair, the hair's Mrs. Kahn's. The same dark color." Mr. Kahn's hair was a businessman gray. "But otherwise, Mr. Kahn, he looks just like you. Like father like son. A striking resemblance."

Having finished off the Kahns, she returned to the

[107]

Oronskys. "Jacob, please, say hello to the man who made it possible."

"Hello," he said reverently, as if talking to God. "I'm glad I could visit Omongo with my wife here."

"Forget it," muttered Mr. Oronsky. "So, Kahn, are you listening? Without the lace trim, he says he couldn't sell those dresses to a *schwartza*. Not even a Puerto Rican . . ."

"Randy," his father got him in a corner, "I don't like to talk about this, but your mother asked me to find out if you been going regular?"

"Going where?"

Mr. Levine put his hands in his pockets. "She asked me to find out whether you been . . . well, having regular habits."

Randy nodded. What habits? He didn't smoke; he didn't drink.

Steiner grinned broadly. "Well, Mr. Oronsky, and Mr. Kahn. What do you think of your fine boys?"

Mrs. Levine stared angrily. Maybe he hadn't seen her. "Hello," she said, blocking his view. Steiner cleared his throat with a slight nod.

"When I first sent our Michael up here, I used to feel guilty," confessed Mrs. Oronsky. "As if I was trying to get rid of him, so my husband and me could have some peace around the house. Now, he doesn't just come because we make him, he comes because he wants to. I think he likes it even better than home." Steiner beamed.

"All the boys get that way," said Mr. Kahn. "They find something here that's missing when they get back home."

"The excitement," said Mrs. Kahn. "Always something to do, some activity."

"It's because we treat them like men," said Steiner. "We offer every one of them the chance to be something, to win."

"It's like business," said Mr. Kahn. "My father thought

it was the worst thing in the world when I left school to earn a few dollars. But it was more than the money. It was the chance to make something of myself."

"For a man without a diploma, my husband has certainly done all right," said Mrs. Kahn, waving her two-and-a-half-carat diamond ring.

"Like *my* husband," said Mrs. Oronsky. "From a factory worker to one of the biggest men in the industry." She motioned with her three-carat diamond ring.

"And that's why," said Mr. Oronsky, excitedly, "above everything else, it should be a profitable business."

Steiner turned pale.

"A house without profit cannot stand," shouted Oronsky.

Steiner reached for a cigarette. He put it back. It wouldn't look right.

Mrs. Levine tried again. "Randy looks pretty good, don't you think?" she said, pointing to her son with her quarter-carat diamond. Jealous, that's what! That she got him here free of charge, that she didn't have to pay a single penny. With all their big talk, they had to pay. Through the nose. Just let him try and collect now. She wouldn't give them one thin dime, not after this treatment. "Randy darling," she cried. He was turning red. "Show Momma around the camp a little before the evening sun goes down." She hustled them down the stairs.

"Jacob, why didn't you talk to him?" she said angrily when they were outside. "You think you're suddenly inferior?"

"Steiner didn't give me a chance. Besides, if I have to pay so Steiner will say a few words, believe me, I'd rather be ignored. His talk I can do without."

"I'd rather pay," muttered Mrs. Levine. "You think I like being different?"

"Doesn't money mean anything to you, Esther? Look how much we saved by getting him in free."

"Save!" she exclaimed. "How can you save when you don't have anything in the first place? In the second place, you didn't get it for free. I won't stand for it, Jacob. Not after all you went through. Not after all that risk."

What risk? Randy was sorry they'd ever come. He'd have been better off if they'd stayed home. He wanted to be like Norman, alone. "Cut it out," he pleaded.

"Tell your father to cut it out." She pushed a tear from each eye.

KITCHEN POLICE

AT DINNER, everyone was so nice. After she'd made Jacob go and threaten Mr. Oronsky with the union unless they could act like decent, democratic men and women. That did it.

"Please, the bread pass," said Mr. Levine, sweetly. Mr. Oronsky did what he was told.

"Such a lovely meal," smiled Mrs. Levine. "I certainly hope what they give my Randy's just as good."

"My boy, too," said Mrs. Kahn.

"Mine, too," said Mrs. Oronsky.

"What do you think," said Mr. Oronsky, "every boy gets a different meal?"

"I have to admit," said Mrs. Levine, "this steak is excellent. Only I can't help feeling it would be better if it was kosher."

"Listen," said Mr. Kahn, "when it comes to meat, you're looking at an expert."

"He owns a chain of supermarkets," said Mrs. Kahn, fingering her diamond.

"Not a chain," said Mr. Kahn modestly, "just two."

"A chain," she insisted. "Two's a chain as much as a hundred."

He lowered his voice to reveal a trade secret. "It's the same meat," he whispered. "Only with the kosher stuff, you have to pay a rabbi. Personally I'm glad they don't keep a kosher kitchen here. If they did, it'd cost us more." He took another bite. He stopped chewing. He remembered. No wonder she wanted them to serve kosher food. For those who didn't pay, only the best!

Mrs. Levine sunk her teeth into the nearly raw flesh. She'd sent it back special; the first one was only medium rare. *Cost us more.* Very clever, that Mr. Kahn: a dig! She ground an artery, extracting the nourishment and savory juices. Daintily, she deposited the remains on the growing heap of chewed steak. Nothing but cartilage, that's what the radio man had told her. *Cost us more.* Another remark like that and she'd make Jacob get up and demand publicly that they be polite or the Levines would leave the table, both of them, immediate, right after dessert.

Pistachio ice cream. Mrs. Levine ordered seconds. The others were too afraid. Mrs. Kahn was telling Mrs. Oronsky about her brand-new ranch-mink stole and Mrs. Oronsky was telling Mrs. Kahn about *her* latest, full-length mutation mink. Mr. Kahn was telling Mr. Oronsky how lousy business was and Mr. Oronsky was telling Mr. Kahn how much lousier *his* business was. Mr. and Mrs. Levine politely excused themselves from the table, he with no business to talk about, she with no mink.

"They could have discussed things we were interested in," she said when they were almost out of earshot.

"What for instance?" asked Mr. Levine.

"Zionism for instance," she said. "Education for instance."

"Since when do you talk about things like that?"

"I think educated people should talk about educated things, not just mink, mink all the time."

"You lost interest in mink? Every year around our anniversary, suddenly that's the main topic of conversation."

"That's different," she said. "Believe me, Jacob, if I had a mink, I wouldn't go brag about it."

"Who said you have a choice?"

"Choice!" she exclaimed. "To have or not to have mink, is not the question. And please, before people take notice, stop this arguing at once. It don't look nice."

Mr. Levine smiled. He tried to look nice.

Mrs. Levine did likewise.

They walked down the aisle, hand in hand, like a newly married couple, through the swinging door, ducking under a tray loaded with empty glasses. They passed a sign with large black letters: NO ADMITTANCE—KEEP OUT—THIS MEANS YOU!

She led the way through the kitchen vapors, guiding him past steaming washers, near smoking stoves, by hissing pots and pans and bubbling kettles, to a huge, fuming cauldron. She got up on the platform and stuck her head in. "Leftover soup," she cried. "The same soup we ate for dinner. I know these tricks. You there. Cook. Hey, cookie. Yoo hoo." A hulking Negro loomed on the horizon. Mr. Levine stepped behind her. "Take me to your meat department." The cook led her to the chopping block. Mr. Levine trailed, ready to run at the drop of an ax.

They paraded past the knives and cleavers to the dishwashing machine. "Colored help," she whispered to her husband. "Cheap, that's why."

[112]

She picked up a dish as the dryer coughed it out. "Jacob, look. How clean the machine gets them! I'm telling you, I couldn't do better myself. Don't touch. You'll get your germs on them. At least he gets to eat on a clean plate." She patted the machine. "Congratulations," she announced. "A job well done."

A sad-looking old man was sitting at a small table. "You shouldn't be eating here," she said harshly. The man shrugged. What terrible manners. He ate as if it were his last supper. "Here," she said, moving his table away. "Isn't that better? Now you can eat without putting your germs on those clean dishes." He smiled gratefully.

"Oh, there you are," she shouted. It was Steiner. "You certainly keep a clean kitchen. That much I have to say. And the meat looks very sanitary. But the soup, why the day-old soup? Why don't you have it fresh every day like a nice restaurant, hm?"

"Mrs. Levine," said Steiner, trying to control himself. "We think we do a good job and we've nothing to hide. But you can't just take it on yourself to march in here and upset all the help." The butcher stood behind, testing the fresh edge of the cleaver with his thumb.

"Well!" she exclaimed. "If that's the way you feel, we'll leave. Me and Mr. Levine never go where we're not wanted."

"Please," said Steiner, "don't make us an exception."

"What's he trying to hide in there? Cockroaches, that's what! He was afraid we'd see one."

Mr. Levine rushed her through the swinging door. "You're talking pretty loud, Esther. Let's get out."

"There he is," she shouted. "Randy darling."

She bent down and kissed him. "Hello, everyone," turning her head in all directions. "Jacob," she said, "look. They're eating the same food as us. The same steak."

"Of course it's the same," said Cohen, indignantly.

"If only Parents' Week would last all season," sighed Mike. "Boy, oh boy."

"Why?" asked Mrs. Levine, frowning. "Why, darling? Don't keep any secrets, please." Mike grinned. "I know," she shouted. "I can guess. When we leave, the food won't be as good. Isn't that what you mean?"

Mel began to laugh.

She turned to the others. They were staring. "You don't mind," she smiled, "if I just whisper a second. It's something I have to tell Randy. Please darling, don't look so embarrassed. They understand."

"We understand," said Mike, nodding solemnly.

"Sure," said Mel, stroking his chin.

"Don't eat the soup tomorrow," she whispered. "It's no good."

Mel picked up three ketchuped French fries in his fingers and slipped them through his teeth. Norman reached for the last roll. Mike beat him to it.

"Don't they have a rabbi to teach these boys good manners?" demanded Mrs. Levine.

"Rabbi? Oh yeah," said Cohen, licking his fingers. "He insists on eating kosher, so Steiner stuck him in the kitchen."

"The kitchen! So that's who that poor old man was. Jacob, did you hear? What a nerve! Where I come from, every rabbi's a king."

"Where's the toilet?" said Mr. Levine, eager to break away.

"Please, Jacob."

"What's the matter? Is toilet a dirty word around here?"

"Just because some people are fresh and don't have manners, doesn't mean, Jacob, you got to be." She looked at Mike and Mel.

"All right," said Mr. Levine. "So where's the damn bathroom?"

[114]

"No," she said. "Rest room. Where's the men's rest room?"

"What are you asking me for? I'm the one who's got to go!"

RECONNAISSANCE

"THIS IS ONE HELLUVA NICE PLACE you got here, Levine," said Norman, as they crawled across the log, carefully, as if hungry crocodiles were gaping in the water below.

"Nobody else even knows about it," said Randy. "It's a secret island."

"You shouldn't have told me," said Greenberg. "Now it ain't a secret any more."

"I don't care about you knowing," said Randy. "Anyhow, the whole idea is sort of stupid. Secrets are kid stuff."

"What I wouldn't give to have a hideaway like this with the gang!" said Norman, looking at the pines to pick a good tree house. He pointed across the blue lake toward the opposite cliffs. "Ever been over there?"

"It's out of bounds," said Randy. "Anyway, the currents are too strong. I tried to get there in my canoe and I had to turn back."

"Even if you made it, the rocks look too steep to climb," said Norman. "What a place for an ambush!"

Randy jumped. "What was that! Sounds like someone coming."

"Aw, cool off. It's just an animal." They crouched together and listened. The snapping of twigs and leaves. "Shh!" warned Norman, pulling Randy closer. "If it's a person, we'll hear it again. They'll want to find out what's happening." Norm threw a stone. Something scurried away.

"It's gone," said Randy.

"I was right," said Greenberg. "A person would have been scared by the rock. He'd have yelled bloody murder."

"Must have been an animal all right," said Randy. "A big one. Maybe a deer." He aimed an imaginary rifle. "Boy, what a trophy a deer's head would make, hanging over my bed."

They walked back to the bridge. This time, instead of crawling, they stomped across, as if they were heroes, as if they'd shot the deer.

"You know what I thought it was at first?" Randy said. "Indians!"

"You're off your rocker, Levine. There's no Indians around here."

Randy picked up a stone and skimmed it across the water. "Maybe."

"What do you mean, 'maybe.' Steiner says the Omongo Indians were wiped out to the last man. Because they were so brave."

"Eagle told me they're living in the forest, waiting to attack," said Randy.

"Attack what?"

"The camp. They want it back. Eagle says they'll come in disguise. They'll scalp every white man in sight. You think he's telling the truth?"

"Who the hell knows?" said Norman. "How am I supposed to be able to tell who's lying and who ain't in a dump like this?"

Randy's stone skipped four times across the water. "I'm real sorry, Norm, about your mom not coming."

Greenberg ripped off a piece of bark. "Look, jerk, I don't need you to feel sorry for me."

"Anyhow, we got to get back for the Grand Inspection."

"I can just hear the Great White Bastard: 'Here's our spotless john,' and, 'Here's where we burn our pure garbage.'" He started to carve a dirty word on the big tree.

"Is she coming up tomorrow?" asked Randy, thinking how lucky Norm was not to have his mother and father around, always yelling at each other.

"Who cares?" said Norman, snapping his knife closed and shoving it in his pocket.

SECRET INTELLIGENCE

STEINER LOWERED HIS RAZOR. He looked at himself in the mirror. The white foam beard made him fantastically ancient, a prophet from the Old Testament.

He began to shave. She'd come. The telegram said so. He'd take her on a special tour, de-luxe, all by herself. What would a few thousand mean to her? Another tax deduction, that's what. The Joyce Greenberg Foundation. Ten thousand dollars. Or should he ask for twenty? Thirty?

A knock at the door. "Come in."

Flinn was out of breath. "Sir," he muttered excitedly. "Mr. Steiner, sir." Flinn panted, trying to get it out. "I saw them. The two of them."

"Who?" said Steiner.

[117]

"Levine, and . . ." he tried to catch his breath, "Greenberg. Way out behind the Mess Hall. While I was looking for a place for the Treasure Hunt."

Steiner gazed into the mirror. He looked good in a T shirt and tennis shorts. At least five years younger.

"I saw them plain as day. I was as close to them as I am to you. I tell you they were . . ." He paused.

"For God's sake, Lieutenant, speak up. I don't have all day."

"They had their arms around each other," he blurted.

"I'm glad Greenberg has *some* friends," beamed Steiner.

"But that wasn't all. They were . . . well . . ."

"Damn it, Flinn, what do you want from me?"

"Well, sir, I could swear it, I know it . . ."

"Enough of your stammering," snapped Steiner, nervously reaching for the doorknob. "I've got to meet the parents."

"They were kissing!"

Steiner sat down. "Get me a glass of water. And one of those tablets." Steiner's hand trembled. The water spilled. He gulped the pill quickly.

"I was trying to say, sir, that I saw them kissing."

They avoided each other's eyes. "And that's not all . . ." Steiner's newly shaven face flushed a light pink. Flinn was pale.

"Do you know what you're saying?" whispered the Great White Father.

"Positive, sir. I swear it. I watched them a full ten minutes."

"Don't tell me," cried Steiner. "I don't want to hear another word." He swallowed some more water. He looked up. "Did they . . ." Steiner hesitated. Flinn flushed. "Did they see you?"

"No, sir. They didn't even know I was watching."

"Listen, Flinn, I've got problems of my own. It's not an easy job running this camp."

"Yes, sir."

"I've got important things on my mind without being bothered by this . . . affair."

"But this *is* important," said Flinn.

"Don't you tell me what's important!" shouted Steiner. "Forget it. It's happened before and it'll happen again and the world's still spinning around."

"You mean you're not even going to punish them?"

"I mean," shouted Steiner, "that you're going to shut up! Especially about the Greenberg boy. I want him handled as if he were a fifty-thousand-dollar bill, as if he were a bankbook with your whole life's savings."

"Whatever you say, Mr. Steiner. You're the boss. Only I don't see why you're so easy on them."

The Great White Father raised his fist. "God damn it," he cried, "who's running this camp, you or me?"

"You, sir," admitted Flinn.

"That's right," shouted Steiner. "This year I'm running Omongo. And I want to be running it next year, too. So you just keep your nose out of things that don't concern you." He lowered his voice. "Maybe, Lieutenant, at the end of the season, you'll get a nice fat bonus."

They shook hands. Steiner held on. "Don't worry," said Flinn, trying to withdraw his fingers, "don't worry, sir."

"A bonus," he repeated. "A big one."

Before Flinn could say more, Steiner marched out, slamming the door.

GRAND INSPECTION

"THIS WAY, PEOPLE," said Rabbi Yeslin, shepherding the flock. They followed him faithfully.

"So nice, isn't he?" said Mrs. Kahn.

"A real charmer," said Mrs. Halpern.

"A learned old man," said Mr. Levine. "I was talking to him a while back. He knows everything there is about the Bible."

"You mean the Old Testament," corrected Mr. Halpern.

"What other Bible is there?" said Mr. Levine.

"The latest of course, the new one."

"I mean the real one," said Mr. Levine, "the original."

"Jacob." Mrs. Levine tapped him on the shoulder. "I'm worried. Where could he be?"

"He's probably running around, getting in shape," said Mr. Levine. "After we leave, there's going to be a big contest. A war. Believe me, I should be so lucky to spend a summer here. I'd lose all this." He pointed to his stomach.

"Me too," said Esther, hesitating to point.

"Me too," said Fat Stuff's mother, turning to smile.

Mrs. Levine nodded. "Jacob," she whispered, "isn't that Mrs. Halpern a wonderful woman? What a fine husband she's got. Shoe business. One of the biggest."

"You don't say."

"Not so loud. You know, our little Randy is certainly

making friends with the right people. What connections. That chubby boy there, that's Mrs. Halpern's son Berney."

"A striking resemblance."

"Now, friends, if you'll go inside please," commanded the rabbi. The arts and crafts shop filled with smoke and people and loud conversation.

"I think it's wonderful," said Mrs. Halpern. "Letting the boys find themselves this way."

"Wonderful," agreed Mrs. Levine. "I wish when I was young, I could have this opportunity to be artistic. I'd be a different personality now, believe me."

"Me, I have my own way to express," said Mrs. Halpern. "Creative shopping."

"With the housework and everything, who has a chance to create?" sighed Mrs. Levine. "I guess maybe you have a maid?"

"A marvelous one," said Mrs. Halpern. "Hannah's been with us for years."

"Lucky, lucky. I can never find the right help."

"Help? Who can afford?" said Jacob.

"My husband," Esther smiled acidly, "always the big joker."

"People! May I have your attention," shouted Yeslin. "Mr. Tannenbaum, our arts and crafts counselor, is, unfortunately, not here. Indisposed. Maybe one of you boys will volunteer to show the parents how to make a pot."

"That would be so interesting," said Mrs. Kahn. "I've bought so many dishes and cups, especially Limoges, I simply love them, but I never even thought about how they were made. Isn't that funny? Someone sells them and you buy them and that's all there's to it. But of course, someone has to make them, too."

"Not so funny," said Mr. Halpern. "If you only knew the work that goes into a plain old shoe . . ."

"No shop talk," groaned Mrs. Halpern. "This is a vacation."

"We're not fooling around with this junk any more," smiled Mike. "We got better things to do."

"Junk? What could be better than being creative, than expressing yourself?" said Mrs. Oronsky, flourishing her hands.

"Mike's right," said Mr. Oronsky. "This is mainly for the little kids. These boys are too old for that."

"You're never too old to learn," said Mrs. Levine. They stared at her.

"Who said anything about being old?" said Mr. Oronsky.

"You did," shouted Mrs. Levine. So maybe he was Jacob's boss. But up here they were all created equals.

"I was referring to the boys," said Mr. Oronsky. "I didn't mean us. Of course none of us is old."

"How could your son be old and you not?" reasoned Mrs. Levine. "It's not logic."

"Now people, walk around and have a good look. This clay business is very important. In the Bible it says . . ."

"That's enough." Everyone turned. The Great White Father stepped into the room. "You can go back now."

"Don't make him leave us," said Mrs. Levine. "He's been so gracious."

"Yes," seconded Mrs. Halpern. "A lovely man."

Steiner looked around, at the Kahns, the Oronskys, the Halperns ganging up on him. "O. K.," he said. "Stay!" He nodded angrily at Yeslin.

"I want to see what they made," said Mr. Halpern.

Fat Stuff pointed to the closet with the huge padlock. "It's over there, Pop. Inside."

"What are you ashamed of?" said Mrs. Halpern. "You think we're going to compare you with Mozart?"

"That's a different field," said Mr. Halpern.

[122]

"What do you think, I'm stupid? Art is art. For it's own sake. Forever," she added. "Please, darling, don't correct so much."

"It's locked," said Fat Stuff, standing by the closet. "He's put a big lock on it."

"Let me see." Mike examined the dials. "That shouldn't be hard to crack."

"Michael!" protested Mrs. Oronsky. "Don't do that. It's not yours."

"It is so," said Mike. "What's in it is mine." He bent over the dial caressingly, trying to hear its heartbeat. Mel looked on with admiration.

"Michael. Shame. Lock-picking," said Mrs. Oronsky.

"How's it coming?" asked Mr. Oronsky.

Steiner collected a crowd near the scrap barrel for his lecture on sportsmanship. He turned his back on the group near the closet.

"Where's the key?" said Mrs. Oronsky.

"It's a combination," whispered Mr. Oronsky.

"Break it," said Fat Stuff.

"Use a hammer," said Mel.

"A blowtorch," suggested Mr. Halpern.

"Herman! Such manners."

Tannenbaum appeared from nowhere. "What's this, vocational training?"

Oronsky gasped. Mike ducked behind his father. His mother stepped in front of both of them. "Leave 'em alone," she said.

"Let's visit the tennis courts," suggested Steiner.

"We've already been there," said Mrs. Levine.

"Then we'll visit the baseball diamonds," said Steiner, forcing a smile.

"The rabbi's taken us there, too."

"The rabbi!" Steiner's voice trembled. "Then the Mess

[123]

Hall," he shouted. "We'll have an afternoon snack." He tried to look pleasant. "Tea!" he cried.

"Any cookies?" asked Mrs. Oronsky, her son's disgrace already forgotten.

"I got hunger pains," said Mrs. Levine.

"Me too," said Mr. Halpern. "Berney, aren't you hungry yet?"

"You bet," said Fat Stuff.

"I'm glad we're getting out of here," said Mr. Oronsky. "This clay makes me sick. Must be the smell." He turned to Sid. "You know," he said, "it smells lousy."

"Sickening, isn't it?" said Sid, clenching his teeth. "You know why this clay stinks?"

"Why, darling?" asked Mrs. Oronsky, letting bygones be gone.

"The manure they used was too fresh."

"Manure!" cried Mrs. Oronsky, rushing to the door. "Henry, I'm going to faint."

"What's wrong? What's the matter?"

"Henry," she said weakly, "I got some on my thumb!"

ENCOUNTER

SID THOUGHT of the years ahead, imagining the dorm was a prison. His crime: wanting a degree. The sentence: four years of poring over lists of French verbs and German generals. He'd like to use the tuition money for his pottery. Not for B's and A's, but for something real, an attic studio in Greenwich Village. Maybe he'd even grow a beard.

The sharp screeching of tires. He folded his copy of *The People's Songbook*. A misty twilight illumined the leaves. He felt homesick. It was quiet, subdued, almost eerie. The door opened.

"Hello." She smiled like the Muse herself, dazzling, but too delicate to touch. "Is this the arts and crafts shop? They told me I'd find my son Norman here."

He nodded. "Whoever told you Norman would be here was trying to be funny."

"Why should they want to fool me?"

"It's an old Omongo custom," said Tannenbaum, bitterly.

She looked around the room. "Arts and crafts. Strange he should be interested in this."

"It's the only thing he doesn't hate," said Sid, wishing he could tell her Norman went for art all the way, body and soul, as *he* did.

"Y' know, he's had every conceivable type of toy. My husband . . ." She paused. ". . . once bought him, last Christmas I think, a whole collection of power tools. But he never used them. Not even once. He's always been like that, indifferent. Funny he should take to this. Something so simple."

"I'm not sure it's simple," said Sid, peevishly.

"I didn't mean it that way. I only meant, well, it's so basic. And what's he made?" she asked cheerfully.

"He's still working on it. He wouldn't want you to see it till it's finished."

"All right," she smiled, sitting down, "then I'll wait."

"You'll have to wait a darn long time, I'm afraid."

She deposited her gum in the clay barrel. "Then, while I'm waiting, I'll make something. It won't hurt my ring will it?"

He'd never seen a diamond so big, not even in a show window. "It washes off."

[125]

"What shall it be?" she asked impishly.

"In this school, the pupil does half the teaching," explained Sid, proudly. "You make what you want."

"All right, Professor, since you're that way, guess what I'm making."

"What do I win?"

"The right to keep it."

Sid chuckled.

"And the duty to help me look for my son."

She formed a large phallus, rolling it like a piece of dough. She added two round lumps.

"I give up," said Tannenbaum, blushing.

"It's not finished," she said, shaping a long oval face.

"An ostrich," he cried with inspiration.

Mrs. Greenberg looked annoyed. "Wait till it's ready." She molded some tiny forelegs hanging uselessly in the air. Then she took the creature's rear and twisted it into a tail.

"Now I really give up."

"A dinosaur, dopey."

"But dinosaurs don't have ears."

"What do you mean?" she said sharply. "How do you think they hear?"

"They're inside," he explained. "They don't have any ear lobes. You lose."

"Tell you what I'll do. I won't lose; but I won't win, either. I'll let you be my guide. The first person we see who looks like a whiz on dinosaurs, we'll walk up and ask." She started on another piece of gum.

Sid gulped. She was unreal, too beautiful. Her lips moved gently, like the fluttering wings of a rare and glittering ceramic bird.

CARNIVAL

▌▌▌▌▌▌▌▌▌▌▌▌▌▌▌▌▌▌▌▌▌▌▌▌▌▌▌

BARKERS, FREAKS, FAT MEN, FORTUNE TELLERS gathered about
in noisy clusters, swirling in front of booths and around the
tables. Steiner grinned at the sign: ALL MONEY TO BE DONATED
TO LOCAL COMMUNITY CHEST.

Near the entrance, a group of parents busy pitching
pennies with anxious, prayer-like gestures. The barker
eagerly raked in the coins with his little wooden hoe. "Try
your luck at Pitch-a-Penny," shouted Fat Stuff Halpern.
"Get it in and we double it."

"Hey," yelled Mr. Oronsky, "how about bringing them
milk bottles a little closer."

"Yeah," shouted his wife, "let us have a chance." She
pitched another penny. It bounced off. "Oy," she frowned,
adjusting her mink stole.

"Maybe you ought to try your hand at something else,"
said Mr. Oronsky. "That makes eighteen cents."

"No, I'll win," she insisted. "If it takes me all night."

"Look," cried Mrs. Kahn proudly. She displayed a coin.
"I won."

"How, darling?"

Mrs. Kahn looked helplessly at her husband. Should she
tell?

Mrs. Oronsky stared, her teeth set in a determined smile.
"How'd you do it?" she repeated.

[127]

"A nickel," muttered Mrs. Kahn. Their faces lit up. "It's heavier," she confessed. "With a nickel it's easy."

Mrs. Oronsky asked her husband for some nickels. "But, Ida, that's five pennies."

"So? I can't count? I don't care if it's ten pennies. It's the weight. You can see a nickel is heavier than . . ."

"All right, leave out the physics." He gave her a handful of nickels.

"Heavier," said Mrs. Kahn, repeating her formula. "Pennies, they're brass. Too light. Now nickels, they're silver. That's why they work. I won on my first try." She pointed to her winnings. "And believe me, I'm no genius."

"You can say that again," grumbled her husband. "Why'd you let them in on it?"

Fat Stuff was putting on weight. The pockets usually reserved for candy bulged. Now and then he would generously deposit a few coins in the cigar box marked BANK, and with his pudgy fingers, dump the remainder into his pockets. Everyone was too busy losing money to notice the real winner, the champ: Fat Stuff Halpern—Croupier, grinning as he raked in eighteen, gave out two. "Step right up, folks. Try your luck," he shouted. "It's all for charity."

"Crowds and noise kind of frighten me," said Joyce, grabbing hold of Sid's arm. "C'mon and be my guide. You decide which way we'll go."

"I'm not used to having slaves," laughed Sid. "I usually let the kids do as they please."

"I'm not a kid, silly. I'm old enough to be your . . . big sister." She pressed his hand. "If it makes you happier, you be the slave."

"As you wish, Your Majesty," he curtsied.

"Not that way," she commanded. "For tonight you may be the King."

Sid smiled. What a sense of humor.

"Come and see the one and only Big Chief Flying

Eagle," shouted Mike Oronsky, decked in an oversized black raincoat, a Homburg which dropped over his forehead, and a black umbrella which he used as a pointer.

"That isn't my little Prince, is it?" asked the Queen.

"No," said the King. "That's one of the Prince's playmates."

They entered the tent of colored blankets, towels and large white sheets.

"And now," said the boy with the Homburg, "Big Chief Flying Eagle will demonstrate his famous war cry."

"Let's get out of here, Your Highness," whispered the King. "He gives me the creeps."

"Mr. Tannenbaum. Tell me frankly, how's my Randy in arts and crafts?"

"Kindly address him as Your Majesty," said the Queen.

"No, we're in disguise," said the King. "They're not supposed to know who we are."

"What's this?" said Mrs. Levine. "A masked ball? Why didn't they tell me? I could have dressed up."

"You could be Esther," said Jake, snickering. "I'll be Haman."

Esther was eying the diamond bracelet. "Lovely costume jewelry," she sighed. The Queen looked insulted.

"And now, ladies and gentlemen," announced the barker, "the famous, ear-piercing, spine-tingling, bloodthirsty war cry of Big Chief Flying Eagle!"

The Big Chief stood stiffly, his face rigid, like a mask hung on a peg. "Get-out-of-here! You-don't-belong-here!"

"What's he mean, I don't belong? I paid," cried Mr. Levine.

"Don't be funny," said Esther. "He's making with the war cry."

"Come and try your luck," yelled a barker. "Catch a fish and you win it."

"No," said Joyce. "I'm not hungry right now."

[129]

"Your Majesty is certainly hard to please," said the King.

"That's been my downfall," said the Queen. "Boredom and fickleness."

"Combined with a smile like the Mona Lisa," said Sid, not quite daring to look at her. She grinned knowingly.

"This is more like it," she said, stopping in front of a Fortune Teller's tent.

Sid couldn't believe it. "But it's just superstition," he explained. "Fortune telling's a lot of hooey."

"My Royal Analyst tells me I have a disgusting enthusiasm for the future and an enthusiastic disgust for the present."

"Analyst?" Sid let go of her hand, shocked.

"Shh," she whispered as they stooped through the tent entrance. "Don't break his trance."

A tall boy was seated ceremoniously on a high stool. He wore a long white beard and a turban made from a towel. "Gimme yer palm," he said. "I see in yer future, in this here line, yer going to come into a lot of money."

"I already have that," she protested.

"I see in yer future a tall, dark, handsome man."

"I guess that leaves me out," said the King.

"Don't be a dope," she laughed. "That's an accurate description of you." Sid blushed.

The seer paused. "That's all."

"Tell me more," she pleaded. She handed him another penny.

"The rest," he assumed a look of gloom, "the rest is darkness."

"If you can't see anything, I want my money back," she snapped.

"Nothing doing. It's in the jar already."

"Then reach for your crystal ball. I want my fortune told," she cried. "That's what I paid for."

[130]

"O.K.," said the boy, reluctantly. "Put out yer hand again."

She exposed her palm. The boy examined it minutely, tracing the paths with his dirty fingernail. "I see a tall, dark, handsome man."

"You already told me that."

"Hold yer horses." He followed a different path. "Danger," he muttered. "Only ya don't know it. A big empty house, and, and . . ."

"What is it?" Her face looked puzzled. Her arm started to tremble. Just slightly. Just enough to make him want to hold it, to steady it.

"What do you see?" she cried.

"Death!" uttered the boy.

"Damn." She jerked her hand back. "Let's get out of here."

Outside, she was smiling. Had she really been upset, really afraid? Was she really having fun? Was she really so beautiful? Was she really a queen?

She held him tightly, affectionately. Or was it mock affection?

"Mrs. Greenberg!" The Great White Father. Sid held Joyce closer. "Delighted to see you, Mrs. Greenberg. When did you arrive?"

"A short while ago."

"I certainly hope you're having a good time," said Steiner, looking at Sid, his smile wavering, disappearing, re-emerging.

"A perfectly lovely time," she said, holding Sid tightly. Sylvia Steiner looked at them, at their bodies, their arms, touching, interlocked.

"Oh!" exclaimed Joyce, suddenly laughing. "I forgot. Mrs. Steiner," she turned, "I have a problem."

"Yes, dear?" said Sylvia, icily.

"Do dinosaurs have ear lobes? Sid says they don't and I say they do."

[131]

The Great White Father looked at Sid with angry eyes, telling him: get out, fast, or else!

"I'm afraid I don't really know anything about dinosaurs," said Mrs. Steiner. "But I'm sure Mr. Tannenbaum must be right. Everything Mr. Tannenbaum says is right."

"Oh, uh, Tannenbaum." Steiner glared at him. "I want to have a talk with you later."

"You're not going to take my guide away?" She looked helpless, like a piece of cheese confronted by a huge rat.

"You're not going to take him away from her, are you, Great White Father Figure?" cried Sylvia. The rat could almost hear the meow of the sex-starved alley cat.

"Sylvia!" shouted Mr. Steiner. She'd gone. "You'll have to excuse my wife," he said, forcing a smile. "The excitement, you know."

A short brawny figure approached. "Cohen. Come here," shouted Steiner. "I want you to meet Mrs. Greenberg and Mr. Tannen . . . What am I doing! You already know each other." His face turned red.

"Pleased to meet you," grinned Tannenbaum.

Cohen stared at their joined hands. So that was it. Tannenbaum was brown-nosing her, trying to cut in on the tip!

"Mrs. Greenberg's been looking for her son." Steiner's smile reasserted itself.

"Norm's in the tent, sir. Confined to quarters along with Levine. For missing the Grand Inspection."

"The night his mother finally gets here, you confine him to quarters!"

"You said you wanted no special privileges . . ."

"That's quite all right," said Joyce Greenberg, democratically. "I *don't* want him to have special treatment." She pulled Sid away.

"Some nice party you're throwing," Oronsky yelled into Steiner's ear, trying to make himself heard over the phonograph. "With a little more fixing, this place would make a dandy gambling casino."

Joyce's ample body felt warm. Not like ceramic at all, but breathing, animate. "Gosh," said Sid. "I feel like a million dollars."

"I haven't had so much fun in years, Your Highness," she smiled, giving him a pinch.

"Never mind the Highness," he said modestly. "Just call me Sid."

They danced in unison, her body dictating his every move. He'd never before danced with anyone who could make the foolish steps into something thrilling. He felt proud. Even if she was taller than him. Their bodies floated past chattering couples, husbands pushing, wives pulling, twisting aside to look at them, whispering. They danced on. Her hand moved to the small of his back. His fingers tightened around her waist. The music grew louder, the laughter more frantic, the winners and losers more angry, more boastful.

"Here he is," cried Cohen, breathless.

Steiner turned. "Hello there, Norm," he gushed. "How's the boy?"

Norman shrugged.

"Come here, pal, I've got a big surprise for you."

Norman looked at him.

Steiner waited. "Don't you want to know what it is?"

Still no answer.

"Your mother!" shouted Steiner. "Your mother, boy! Aren't you happy?"

"Where?" said Norman.

"Where'd she go?" demanded Steiner, turning on Cohen.

"I don't know, sir," said Cohen. "I couldn't watch her and get him, too. I only got so many eyes."

There she was! Norman saw her walking toward the door at the other end of the hall. He started to run.

Cohen grabbed him. "Wait here for your mother."

"Lemme go!" Norman kicked at Cohen's shins.

"I'll break your little neck," said Cohen.

"Lay off him!" shrieked Steiner.

Norm took hold of the game table and dumped it with a loud, metallic clang, scattering the pennies, dimes and broken bottles.

"Ruined," shouted Steiner.

"The money!"

"A quarter."

"Mine."

"Ruined."

"Glass."

"I'm bleeding."

"A nickel."

"Grab it."

"Done for."

They groveled on the floor. Cohen and Norman, the dancers and the barkers and the ticket takers, and Steiner stood above them, a prophet crying in the wilderness: "We're lost! Ruined!"

"Money," they cried.

"Got it."

"Mine! It's mine!"

Casting off their sheepskin cloaks, they scratched and clawed, snarled and spit, fathers at wives, counselors at parents, mothers at sons.

"The money," they chanted. "Gimme! Gimme!"

EXHIBITIONS

||||||||||||||||||||||||||||||||||||||||||||||||||

MR. ORONSKY WAS SILENT.

"Cheer!" whispered his wife. "He's on the same team as Michael."

"Hit," grunted Mr. Oronsky. "A home run let's see."

Randy stepped up to bat.

"I don't understand," said Mrs. Levine. "What's the purpose?"

"Watch the plate," snapped Mr. Levine. It looked like a pillow case that needed a good washing. "Keep your eyes peeled on Randy," he ordered.

"I'm peeling."

"Strike one!"

"Don't!" pleaded Mr. Levine. "No more strikes."

"Strikes?" said Mrs. Levine.

"Don't you know what a strike is yet?" cried Mr. Levine.

Oronsky turned worriedly. "No union threats, Levine."

Mr. Levine bit his lip. "A homer," he shouted. "For your father."

"Jacob, you're making a fool of yourself. I wish him success, too. But a little modesty, please."

"Honey baby," Mrs. Greenberg placed her arms around Norman's waist, "would you be awfully hurt if I left you for a while? It's silly watching a game I don't know anything about."

"You'd be a dope to hang around," said Norman, hiding his disappointment.

"Greenberg," shouted Gans, "you're up."

"Bye-bye, darling." She kissed him on the cheek.

"Remember," whispered Gans, "throw it nice and easy like the Great White Father said."

"Ball one!"

"Hit a homer," yelled Mrs. Kahn. "A homer," she kept shouting, until Mel told her she was expecting too much. "A single, Norman dear," she cried. "Anything."

"Kill 'im," yelled Mr. Halpern. "Pitch it so hard he won't know where it came from."

A slow, easy ball floated over the plate. Norman swung. A chorus of groans.

"Ball four!" The field was silent. Norm took his base indifferently.

The last batter struck out. Groans of rage and outrage. The Iroquois parents cheered.

"Too darn bad," said Randy.

Norman looked up. "About what?" The guy didn't even seem sorry. As if he was in a dream world.

"About your not hitting the ball, of course," said Randy, glumly.

"F' Christ's sake, Levine, is that all you ever think about?"

"But he deliberately walked you," cried Randy. "Didn't you see how easy he was pitching? He made a darn fool of you."

Norman laughed.

"All right, pretty-boy," barked Flinn, "get yourself over to the wrestling match. On the double."

"Television I can understand, but here it's too real," said Mike's mother.

"I suppose it's not real on TV," said Mr. Oronsky, smiling tolerantly.

"Grown men, that's different. This is with little children. Anyhow, TV you can turn off."

"Get it out of your head that our Mike's a little child, Ida. Comes a war, they'll take him like everyone else. And if there's no war to go to, in a few years he'll get married. Let him learn how to protect himself."

"Henry," she looked around to make sure no one was listening. "Have you talked to him yet?"

The campers were drawing lots from Lieutenant Flinn. The parents protested. Their boy was too little for that one; that boy was too heavy for theirs.

"No," whispered Mr. Oronsky. "I'm waiting. Let Steiner make the approach."

"I agree," she whispered. "Let him get desperate."

"I've been looking this place over," said Mr. Oronsky. "It'll make some resort."

"Don't think about it," said Mrs. Oronsky. "You'll get too excited."

"Don't worry," he said. "I can be excited on the inside but outside, cool as a dill pickle. Steiner probably thinks I forgot all about our talk last spring. I know his finances. He'll come running soon."

"Think of those free vacations. 'The Family Oronsky is pleased to present The Omongo Pines.' That's what we'll call it, huh?" Her gold-capped teeth sparkled brightly in the sun.

"Look who's getting excited now," he laughed, pressing her in the ribs.

"Lovely couple," whispered Mrs. Kahn, eying them. "I hear he's one of the biggest in the dress business."

"Watch the wrestling," said Mr. Kahn.

"When Mel wrestles, believe me, then I'll watch. A woman isn't interested in anything but her own family."

"Oronsky," hollered Steiner.

"We were just talking about you, Ida and me." They smiled.

Steiner whispered nervously into Mr. Oronsky's ear. "When you get a chance, come and see me. I'd like to have a talk with you." He paused, then, reluctantly: "It's important."

"Certainly," grinned Mr. Oronsky. He took hold of Ida's hand and squeezed. She squeezed back. "Kill him," he shouted, turning to the wrestlers. Steiner walked away, stopping now and then to wave, to smile, to cheer. It was all mechanical. The Oronskys knew.

Mike was on top of Norman. Lieutenant Flinn was down on the ground, trying to get a better look. Steiner groaned. What kind of public relations was this! Was this a way to win her, by having her son humiliated, beaten, maybe even hurt!

"Stop it!" he demanded. "The fight's over." He stepped into the ring.

Mike was still holding him. Norman refused to quit. "But his elbows, sir. They haven't touched," insisted Flinn.

"For God's sake, break them up," shouted Steiner.

Oronsky strutted into the ring. "Let 'em fight it out. Why coddle 'em?"

Mike squeezed tighter. His knees jammed angrily into Greenberg's thighs, pinning them down hard. Norm's eyes were still open; his face expressionless; his right elbow up, still up off the ground.

"I'm not coddling," shouted Steiner. "But time's up." He pointed to his chronometer.

Flinn grabbed Mike around the waist and pulled him off Norman.

"Not so hard," cried Mrs. Oronsky. "He's my son."

"Congratulations, fella," shouted Mr. Oronsky, pumping Mike's hand. "Far as I'm concerned, time or no time, you won." He looked at Steiner bitterly.

[138]

"Did he hurt you?" asked Mrs. Oronsky, timidly.

"Him!" shouted Mike. He pointed to Norman, still lying on the ground. "That guy couldn't hurt a fly."

"It wasn't fair, Norm," whispered Randy. "He's heavier than you." He helped brush off the dirt. Was that blood? Maybe Norm had really been hurt. "Let me fight Oronsky," shouted Randy.

Flinn was wiping the dust off his knees with a handkerchief, as if polishing the outside of a gun.

"Go ahead, Mike," said Mr. Oronsky, pushing him back into the ring. "My kid's still game."

"My boy can do as good as any one else," cried Mrs. Levine, not to be outdone.

"You watch, Ma, I'll beat him," said Randy.

Mr. Levine shrugged. None of his business. Let them fight among themselves, the old American way. But what if Randy won! How would that look? The boss's son, beaten by an employee, a guest. Mr. Levine looked worried.

The contestants eyed each other fiercely. The parents tried to look polite. Flinn stepped to the center. "Ready." They crouched. "Go!"

"Go!" repeated the Oronskys.

"Go!" repeated Mrs. Levine.

At first they were careful, afraid to move, to be tricked, grabbed, to be downed in one quick, humiliating clasp.

Why be so polite? "Bend his arm," cried Mrs. Levine. "Give it everything you got." That broke the spell.

"Get him by the neck!" shouted Mr. Oronsky.

"Choke him," encouraged Mrs. Levine, spreading her arms out like a noose. Mr. Oronsky gave her a dirty look.

Randy was on top. "Break his elbows," shouted his mother.

"They're not supposed to break," whispered Mr. Levine. "They're supposed to touch the ground."

"So touch," she screamed.

[139]

"Esther, please, not so loud."

"Why not?" she shouted. "Because it's your boss's son? I'll shout all I want. It's a free country. Strangle him!"

"Use your knees," yelled Oronsky.

"That's not legal," warned Mr. Kahn.

"Never mind legal. Use the knees."

"Bite him," cried Mrs. Levine.

"The scholarship," whispered Jake. "Don't you want to get it next year?"

Mrs. Levine looked at him.

"Kick him. Kick him," shouted Mrs. Oronsky.

Suddenly Mrs. Levine was no longer shouting. The Levines stared at the ground.

"Your knees," shouted Mrs. Oronsky. "Your nails, your teeth, your head. Use your head."

Mike's face puckered like a rotten apple; his eyes were floating out of their sockets; his skin was turning a deep, blood-colored red. Flinn smiled.

"A dollar!" shouted Oronsky. "Five! Win!" He waved it in the air.

"You hear?" shouted Mrs. Oronsky. "Your father, your own father, giving five dollars."

Flinn sprang up. "The winner," he shouted, "Levine." Mike lay on the ground, stunned.

Mrs. Levine ran up. "Michael dear," she cried. "Are you all right?"

"Nice try," shouted Mr. Levine, grabbing hold of Mike's hand. "Congratulations."

Was his old man crazy! Randy stared.

"No fair," cried Mrs. Oronsky, indignantly. "He used his nails."

"If Randy did that, he apologizes," said Mrs. Levine.

"Ma!"

"What do you mean *if?*" said Mrs. Oronsky, angrily. "Bruises. All over. Illegal."

"Then *I* apologize," said Mrs. Levine.

"Come on," grumbled Mr. Oronsky, thrusting the money back in his pocket, "let's get out of here."

"We'll go, too," said Mrs. Levine. "Mike darling, please take care. Use some alcohol, dear. Rubbing."

The next fight had already begun. The parents were cheering.

"Kick 'im."

"Gouge 'im."

"Twist 'im."

"Listen," cried Mike, when their parents were gone, "what was the big idea?"

"What idea?"

"I mean winning like that."

"Are you kidding!" cried Randy.

"At least you could have made it a draw. You knew my parents were watching."

"So were mine."

"Yours! You didn't even pay to come here."

Randy looked at them trailing after the Oronskys like little squirrels. Why hadn't they cheered like the others? Maybe Mike was right. Maybe they weren't as good.

"You think you belong here, that you're one of us, don't you? Well get this, squirt: the only reason you're here is because of my dad. Why do you think my pop picked you for the scholarship?"

"Because he knows mine, that's why," said Randy. "Because they're friends."

"Friends! Cut that shit, buster. The reason you got picked is because your old man did mine a favor."

He was grinning. Randy looked away.

"You want to know what the favor was?"

Randy said nothing.

"He's a spy."

"What the heck are you talking about?"

[141]

"He reported every single thing at the union meetings, everything that went on. My dad gave the scholarship as a bribe. You know, like Benedict Arnold. Because your old man was such a damn good traitor."

"It's not true," cried Randy. "You made it all up."

"Ask him," smiled Mike. "Ask your old man. See if I'm lying."

"Scratch 'im," they yelled.

"Slug 'im," they screamed.

"Whip 'im."

"I will," cried Randy. "I will."

SAFETY FIRST

"NOTHING'S MORE IMPORTANT than safety," said Mrs. Oronsky, fussing with her lipstick. "That's why I'm telling you they should be wearing life preservers."

"Don't be ridiculous," said Mr. Oronsky. "Imagine trying to paddle a canoe wearing a clumsy life preserver."

"There's nothing to worry about, Mrs. Oronsky," said Steiner. "Our canoes are unsinkable."

"If they're so unsinkable, why are you giving them safety tests, will you please answer that one?"

"I hope our Berney is safe," said Mrs. Halpern. "You know he's pretty heavy. Are you sure that little boat would stay afloat if it tipped over and he had to hang on?"

"I agree." They turned. It was Mrs. Levine. "Too dangerous. Too small."

"That's because they're so far out," said Mr. Levine, trying to reassure her, holding her around the waist, as far as his arm could reach.

"Then they should have the test closer to shore," insisted Mrs. Levine.

"But there'd be no danger at all," said Steiner. "They wouldn't even try."

"See. There *is* danger," cried Mrs. Levine.

"So is your standing here dangerous, at the edge of this pier," said Steiner. "Any minute you could fall in and drown."

The ladies stepped back.

"Business is dangerous, too," said Mr. Halpern. "If I made a few thousand shoes with a single weak stitch, don't you think the Brooklyn Bootery would go bankrupt?"

"You think," said Mr. Levine, "if business got bad, the boss wouldn't lay me off?"

"Now, now," said Mr. Oronsky. "We can always use a good man like you, Jake."

"Still, if you were forced to, you'd have to, right?"

"Enough," whispered Mrs. Levine, giving him a kick. "Don't give him ideas."

"Am I too late?" Mrs. Steiner adjusted the strap of her skin-tight chartreuse bathing suit. The men stared. The women frowned. Sylvia smiled.

"I'm so afraid," said Mrs. Halpern, turning to her husband. "Berney's so heavy."

"A lovely boy he is," said Mrs. Levine. She'd heard Mr. Halpern was one of the biggest shoe manufacturers in New York. Who knew? Maybe he'd give her a discount.

"The race," shouted Mr. Levine. "Stop talking so much."

"I'll put a dollar on Mel," said Mr. Kahn.

"Two dollars says Mike takes it."

"No," shouted Steiner. "It's no race. It's a safety test."

[143]

Everyone groaned. Mrs. Halpern closed her alligator handbag. "Are you sure?" said Mr. Oronsky, putting back his billfold.

"He's positive," said Mrs. Steiner. "Absolutely positive. That schedule and him are like a pair of clocks." They stared at her. Steiner smiled nervously.

On the other side of the lake, near the rocks, so far away they could hardly see, the Intermediates struggled with their boats.

"F' Christ's sake, Norm," shouted Randy, trying to get a grip. "The water's cold. Heave." Norman clung to the sides. That was enough, to hang on, to stay up. Randy's end lifted out of the water, then snapped back.

"Come on, Norm," he yelled. "I can't do the whole thing myself."

"Only one canoe left," said Mr. Oronsky. "It couldn't be Mike."

"Who can see that far?" said Mrs. Kahn.

"I know. It's not him."

"It's not our Mel," said Mr. Kahn.

"Not our Randy," said Mrs. Levine.

"Whose is it?"

"A ghost ship," whispered Mr. Oronsky.

"Don't ask me," said Mrs. Halpern.

"Search me," said Mr. Halpern.

"Why don't you search me," whispered Sylvia, just loud enough so Steiner wouldn't think she was teasing.

"One boy's helping the other climb in."

"Illegal," shouted Mr. Kahn.

"A crime," said Mrs. Levine, "against nature."

"He's taking hold of him with his hands," shouted Mr. Levine.

"Jacob, what are you, the announcer?" She knew. It was him! "Stop it!" she screamed. "He's not ours."

"Certainly not ours," said Sylvia. Steiner shriveled.

"Leave me alone," cried Norman, swallowing water. "I can do it myself."

"They're all waiting," shouted Randy. "You want us to look like jerks?" Norman crooked his arm over the side. With one tremendous effort, Randy lifted him in. Norman sprawled across the bottom. "What the hell's wrong now?" shouted Randy angrily.

"Swallowed too much." His body lay crumpled like a water-soaked rag.

Randy looked at him. "You sure you're O.K.?" Norman answered with a muffled choking. He grabbed the side of the canoe. The beet-red, lettuce-green, lambchop-brown puke tumbled out over the side, churning, diffusing, contaminating the once clear water.

LOVE ON THE ROCKS

THEIR WET BODIES emerged from the pure, cold pond, pressing together, their lips, their tongues, no longer instruments of speech, were red daggers of love, thrusting, exploring. "I really go for you," whispered Sid, his lips brushing behind her ears, down her stolid neck.

"Stop tickling," said Joyce, breaking away. "Anyhow, I'm hungry." She pulled the towel from his waist and began rubbing briskly. Sid grabbed his briefs and dropped them in his lap.

"Grow up," she smiled, snatching the shorts, and tossing them into the bushes.

He wrapped the towel around her face.

"Help, help!" she exclaimed, her voice lost in the folds of rough cloth.

"Do you surrender?"

He spread the moist, cool towel. "Now stop peeking," he said, stretching out on his stomach. She lay down beside him.

"I'm having so much fun, Sid, honey baby." They were a couple of romantics, side by side for the first time on a brand-new sheet. Underneath the whiteness, the honeymoon bed was hard, uneven, a rock. The tin-foil sun headed toward the tips of the trees. It was getting dark.

"I suppose tomorrow you'll be going," he said bitterly.

"Sid, doll, you're shivering." She opened a box of dietetic crackers.

"Parents' Week will be over before we know it," he complained.

"That's always the way," without giving it a thought.

"Would you stay longer? I mean if you could."

"Sure thing. I could spend the whole summer with you," she said, running her hand across his bare back.

"That feels great." He turned over.

"Sid! Don't you ever think of anything else?" she teased, grinning.

He sighed. "I wish I could paint a picture of all this."

"The two of us? Undressed? Shame on you, Sid."

"Not us—all this joy, this happiness, our being together, enjoying each other. And the pond and the dying sun and this big, beautiful rock and those high trees. I'd like to express it all in one grand masterpiece." He ran his fingers along her warm, nude body. "You're lucky." He kissed her hand. "Woman are *expected* to be creative. It's their function."

"What do you mean?" she asked innocently, offering him a cracker.

[146]

"Women are expected to bear children. It's even called that. Procreation. It's become deified. The Virgin Mary outshining Christ."

She looked puzzled.

"Look, when a kid's born, there're all sorts of celebrations, parties, gifts. How many celebrations are there when a symphony is born, when a painting is completed . . ."

"Help me hitch up my bra, will you?"

". . . when a vase is taken out of the kiln?"

She struggled to get dressed. He took hold of her. Their fingers twined. He studied her firm breasts, the small nipples, the smooth torso, the feathery down between her legs, all aglow from the sun, filtering through the forest of branches, red, green, gold, like an inspiring mosaic. "I love you, Joyce!" he blurted. She dropped the brassière.

He attached his mouth to hers. He grew taut like a drawn bow, the string tight, vibrating, the arrow poised. They were breathing in unison, as if they were one, with a single mouth, a single heart. The rhythm became faster, more intense; the bow strained to the breaking point; the string quivered; the arrow warmed, suddenly shooting. In India, a beggar collapsed of hunger; in a jungle thicket, an explorer was caught in the embrace of a cobra; in a courtroom, a glib lawyer pleaded for the life of a killer; in a gold-domed legislature, two gold-toothed, gold-braided generals begged for a war of annihilation; and high above the sterile pond, above the dead, volcanic rock, and the struggling lovers, in a gray unzipped sky a heavy cloud hung limply like the phallus of a fat god about to urinate.

DEBATE

|||||||||||||||||||||||||||||||||||||||||||||||||

"LOOKS LIKE RAIN," said Mrs. Levine.

"I'm glad it didn't rain when they were out in those canoes," said Mrs. Halpern.

"It made me nervous," confessed Mrs. Levine. "I tried not to show it, but it made me very nervous."

"The trouble with us," said Mrs. Halpern, "we don't expect enough from our children. You should have seen Berney before I started sending him here. A regular sissy. My husband could never get him to play with the other boys. He always used to stay inside, even on the sunniest days, with that stupid chemical set. This is Berney's fourth year here and the change! You'd never think he used to be a bookworm. Sending Berney to camp is one of the smartest things we've ever done."

"I'm glad, too," said Mrs. Levine. "I want Randy to learn that the world's no joy ride. Right, Mrs. Halpern? Sink or swim."

"Right," said Mrs. Halpern. "No one's going to help a drowning ship. It's too bad, but that's the way the world is and you may as well get used to it."

"You know," said Mrs. Levine, "sometimes I think the world's a terrible place."

"Certainly it is," said Mrs. Halpern. "But what can you do except try to keep your head above water?"

The dark cloud swelled like a tumor. Mrs. Halpern looked up. "I could have sworn I just saw a plane go by."

"Over here?"

"Yes. And you know what I think it was doing?"

"What?"

"Trying to make rain," said Mrs. Halpern.

"Really?"

"Trying to make rain for the farmers."

"Can you imagine," said Mrs. Levine. "Nowadays these science people can do everything."

"It's terrible. There's nothing left any more for people to do," said Mrs. Halpern. "It's all science, science. Look." She lifted her hand. "I usually don't tell anyone, but look at this ring."

"Beautiful!" exclaimed Mrs. Levine. "Simply beautiful. A star sapphire."

"A fake," whispered Mrs. Halpern, looking around to make sure no one was listening.

"Really!" gasped Mrs. Levine.

"It's made in a factory."

"What'd I tell you, science does everything."

"Take that bracelet you're wearing." Mrs. Halpern pointed to a wristful of glittering stones. "It'd take an expert to tell the difference between those and real diamonds."

"Thank you," smiled Mrs. Levine, flattered. "Anyhow, isn't it stupid for a bunch of grown men to dig little diamonds with their hands when you can so easily make them?"

"But then they're not real," said Mrs. Halpern. "That's my point."

"Real, not real, nowadays what's the difference?"

The two ladies stood against the railing, their painted faces staring at the darkening sky, their plastic teeth chatting, their perfumes drowning out the odor of flowers which lay trampled beneath their neolite soles. Mrs. Levine brushed some pollen off her coal-tar dress. "It's starting to rain."

"We'd better go inside," said Mrs. Halpern.

"I'll bet it's not even real," said Mrs. Levine. "I'll bet it's something that airplane just made."

They stepped under the roof of the porch.

"You know what I hear?" said Mrs. Halpern. "I hear they even got a new way of producing babies. In a test tube."

"You don't say?"

"They're afraid to make it public. If they did, just think what would happen."

"What would be so terrible?"

"You could go to the department store and buy one," said Mrs. Halpern. "Bargain-basement babies. You could call up and have them deliver one C.O.D. You wouldn't even know which babies were real. Half the people in the world would be fakes, artificial, like those diamonds of yours."

Mrs. Levine fingered her expensive rhinestones. "Test-tube babies. It sounds like a good idea. What do you mean, they wouldn't be real? Of course they would. As much as you and me."

"Maybe I'm just old-fashioned," said Mrs. Halpern, sadly.

"Just a little," said Mrs. Levine. "I don't like to say it, but I think you are. Frankly, I think you're a pessimist." She ran her fingers down the sharp, bright cubes of her bracelet. "Real," murmured Mrs. Levine, absent-mindedly.

"What?" said Mrs. Halpern.

"Nothing," said Mrs. Levine. "Nothing."

FISH STORY

▋▋▋▋▋▋▋▋▋▋▋▋▋▋▋▋▋▋▋▋▋▋▋▋▋▋

"IT WASN'T A REAL RACE," said Mr. Kahn, jerking his line along the surface, dangling the bait in front of the starving fish, trying to lure them to their death. "They should have made it official. Then I would have cheered more. Why didn't he give 'em a medal?"

"It's not that easy. You have to win a helluva lot of races before you get an award around here. Steiner don't give them away for nothing. Someday, you should drop over and take a look at Mike's medals. If he wins any more, I won't know where to put them."

"I got the same problem," said Mr. Kahn.

"Listen to what my kid won just last year," said Mr. Oronsky, "a first in tennis . . ."

"Ridiculous game," said Mr. Kahn.

"Let's see you play if it's so ridiculous."

Mr. Kahn gave another pull. The fish refused.

"We got a first in baseball," continued Oronsky.

"So did everyone else on the team."

"Then we got a medal in riflery."

"First?"

"For Mike, a second don't exist."

Kahn stared at the empty line.

"What did *you* win?" smirked Mr. Oronsky.

"Who can keep track? And they're gold, too. Believe me. I had them appraised by my attorney. Nothing but gold." His line grew taut. "Got one," he shouted. He wound it in: a struggling piece of silver.

"Crummy perch," said Oronsky, bobbing his own line angrily, trying to even the score.

"Nine inches if it's a day," said Mr. Kahn, ripping the hook from the half-dead fish.

"Not an inch over seven," cried Mr. Oronsky.

"So? And where's your big fish, wise-guy?"

Oronsky was stumped. He'd get even if he had to stay here all night. Not only would he catch one, but it would be bigger than Kahn's. Not only would it be bigger, but it would have to be gold, all gold, solid.

Kahn rebaited his hook. With a great flourish, he dumped the line back into the water.

"Don't you even know how to cast yet?"

"I don't know how to cast," said Mr. Kahn. "I only know how to catch fish."

For a while they said nothing. The cloud grew larger. The lake shivered in its shadow.

"They're not biting," said Mr. Oronsky. "Something's wrong with this lake."

"What are you talking about?" said Mr. Khan.

"It's the truth. A few years ago, all you had to do is throw in your hook and in a couple of minutes, out came a fish. A big one too. Not like the baby you just got."

"Baby!" Mr. Kahn pointed to the skinny piece of silver lying lifeless on the rock. "That's a full-grown perch."

"If you'd fished here a few years ago, you'd know what I'm talking about."

"What's wrong?"

"It's polluted."

"Up here? Impossible!"

"I'm not kidding," said Mr. Oronsky. "Look at it. You call that water clean?"

The lake darkened. Its surface glimmered like an antique mirror, stained and cracked.

"You think maybe it's dangerous to swim here?"

"That's just what I was thinking," said Oronsky. "Old man Steiner's let this camp slide. Little by little, it's been going downhill. Small things, like that tree in the middle of the Parade Grounds. Steiner swore he'd have it chopped, but it's still there. That's what I mean. Little things: the lake not so clean any more; the medals not so big."

"No kidding," said Mr. Kahn. "I never even noticed."

"Sure. No one else has, either. That's how Steiner gets away with it."

"From now on, I'll keep my eyes open."

"You know," said Oronsky, as if it had just occurred to him, "you know what's wrong with Omongo?"

"What?"

"Steiner don't get all the potential out of the place. Of course the guy's only a schoolteacher, so he probably don't know any better. Listen, Kahn, if I had Omongo, I'd milk it dry."

"How?" said Mr. Kahn, looking into the water. Maybe it was true. Maybe the lake really was polluted. Then maybe his fish . . . Of course. His fish would be diseased. He wound the line in. Why catch a disease?

"First," said Mr. Oronsky, "I'd change the business of the fees. I'd have the same basic fee to cover the same number of weeks. Maybe even lower it a little. You know, to get them to bite."

"You mean the way they're not biting on your hook?" joked Mr. Kahn.

"Yeah. Hey, that's a good one." Oronsky laughed hoarsely. He looked at the fish lying at Kahn's feet. Nine inches! You couldn't sell that thing for a sardine. "Well," he continued, "after I got them to bite, then I'd take them for all they were worth. I'd slap on a dozen different extras.

An extra fee for horseback riding, an extra fee for the overnight hike, an extra fee for special swimming lessons or for skin-diving. Hell, I'd even make them pay extra for doubles. Special meals. Why not? Why should every kid have to eat the same thing?"

"Because it's a democracy," said Mr. Kahn.

"You mean a dictatorship. That's what it is when every kid got to eat the same thing, a dictatorship. Mine's the democratic way. Freedom of choice. And not only meals. I'd have plenty of other things, too. Specially built canoes for those who could afford them. Can't you just see it? Every mother would want her little kid to have just as good a boat as the next kid, just as many extra tennis lessons, just as many special steak dinners. The parents would compete with each other to make sure their sons had nothing less than the others were getting. They'd even want to go them one better. One more steak dinner. One more overnight hike. They'd be fighting to outdo each other. Free Enterprise. Democracy. What a gold mine. And believe me, I wouldn't have any four-day Parents' Week, either. Hell, no. I'd let them stay for the whole summer. But here's the catch, I'd make them pay for it. And I'd make sure each kid knew just exactly how much. Whether his parents were renting a small double or a suite. With a view or just facing a wall. It's all psychology. It's not what people get that counts. It's what they think they're getting. I'd sell them something they'll pay more for than anything else in the world—prestige. I'm telling you Kahn, just let me have this camp for one season. The place would be rolling in dough." He rubbed his palms, counting the take.

"Sounds O.K.," said Mr. Kahn.

"If only I could talk some sense into Steiner. Trouble is, he don't realize that running a camp is a business, like anything else."

"Well, maybe a little different."

[154]

"Different? Everything's a business today. What do you think medicine is? Something to do with saving mankind and all that crap? Hell no, it's for profit. What d'you call the A.M.A.? A union, a high-class union. And the doctors, they don't know? Of course they do. They love it. What do you think politics is, something noble and highfalutin?"

Kahn shrugged. "I don't know, I . . ."

"Of course not. It's a business, same as anything else. You invest the money, you advertise, and you win the votes. Take all this college baloney. Let me tell you, pal, it's one hell of a good business those college people got. Take a look at their fees, what it takes to buy an education. It makes you sick. Everything's a business. What do you think all those gold-striped admirals and generals are, heroes? Don't let anyone kid you. They're businessmen, like you and me. Their business is to look big. What do you think government people are, public servants?"

Mr. Kahn scratched his head.

"You know what their business is? Squeezing money out of the taxpayer."

Kahn nodded. "You got a point there."

"Everything, Kahn, everything. Rabbis, you think they're way above it? Hell, no. When it comes time to make a touch, to ask for a donation, to pass the hat around, believe me, they're just as good businessmen as you or me."

"Better," said Kahn. "You should see the one we got."

"Take my wife."

Kahn turned away.

"Always making a big deal out of culture. You know, music, books. What d'you think, these artists don't know what's going on in the world? Hell they don't. Listen, I saw a colored movie about this artist nut who cut off his ear. Why do you think he did it, because he was feeling sorry for himself? Sure, that's what my wife thought. Let me tell you, pal, you got to read between the lines. He cut off his ear because he wanted publicity. Because his pictures weren't selling so good. You know what I mean? He had a slow-moving item. Like in your grocery when you can't get the baked beans to sell. What do you do? You publicize 'em, right? So that's what this guy does. He cuts off his ear right in front of everyone and first thing you know, they're all talking. Next thing you know, his pictures are selling like hot cakes. Even my wife bought one. Flowers or something. What made her buy it? I'll tell you. She bought it because that artist guy knew how to sell himself."

"When it comes to moving dead merchandise, I know what you mean," said Mr. Kahn, springing to life. "In the grocery business, that's one of the biggest headaches."

"In our business, too," said Mr. Oronsky.

"Say, my wife tells me that Levine character works for you. Is that right?"

Oronsky shrugged. "What can you do? Labor's hard to get."

"Isn't he related to you or something? That's what my wife . . ."

"Related!" Oronsky laughed. "He's a worker. An employee. A sort of labor advisor, if you know what I mean."

"You got a guy just for that?"

"Not exactly. He's a wheel in the union and he sort of keeps me advised on what those union jerks are up to. So I reward him." He winked. "I pull a few strings and I get old Steiner to give the guy's son a scholarship."

"I got to hand it to you. You sure know your way around."

"What do you think, Tri-umf Frocks is so big 'cause I'm dumb?"

"You boys catch any fish yet?" It was the Great White Father.

Oronsky smiled. Why look anxious? Let Steiner make the first move.

Steiner smiled back. The hell with Oronsky. Tonight was the night. He'd meet Mrs. Greenberg right after the banquet. What was money to her? He was saved. He felt it in his bones.

"What do you think of this fish?" said Mr. Kahn proudly.

"Nice one, nice one." Steiner continued on his way, smiling, humming a tune.

It was all on the outside. Oronsky was sure of it. Inside he was dying. What pride could do to a man. He hurled the line.

"You still trying?" said Mr. Kahn.

"Why not? Maybe out there, it's not so polluted." If Kahn could get one, so could he. "Say," said Oronsky, casually, "what the hell are you using for bait?"

"A piece of steak from last night."

He stared at him. "Did you say steak?"

"What's the matter?" asked Kahn, no longer smiling.

"Nothing."

"Tell me."

"I don't want to spoil your fun."

"Tell me!" shouted Kahn.

"Hell, it's just that it's illegal," he grinned.

Kahn stopped moving his rod. "Who said so?" he whispered.

"The New York State Game Laws," shouted Oronsky.

"I, I . . ." His line twitched.

"The laws says, the guy who catches you using that kind of bait gets the reward. Fifty bucks."

"Fifty bucks!" He raced the reel, trying to get away, to escape. He could see the gleam in Oronsky's eyes. Fifty bucks was fifty bucks. "Don't say anything," begged Kahn,

trying to look innocent as he yanked off the bait and tossed
it frantically into the woods. "Please, my wife. Hey, pal,
come on. Please, Oronsky, don't!"

Oronsky looked at him greedily.

HUG ME TILL I DIE

THE JUKE BOX BEGAN:

You can whip me, you can kick me,
You can throw me on the floor,

But Daddy, Daddy, Daddy,
Oh, I'll only love you more.

"That's from the movie," said the soda jerk, handing
them the mimeographed menus.

But Daddy, don't stop, Daddy,
Even if I gotta cry . . .

"What'll it be, folks?" asked the soda jerk.

She squeezed his hand. "I'm going to treat you to a
great big ice-cream sundae, even if it *is* against my diet."

On cue, the soda jerk stepped forward: "There's the
Standard Bearer—scoop of ice cream, syrup and walnuts;
the Adirondack Special—two dips, syrup, walnuts, whip
cream, and a red cherry; then the Star Spangled Glory—
three dips, same thing with fruit; but if you're really
looking for something good, why don't you try the Sweetheart Banana Barge."

"That's it," she said excitedly, "the Sweetheart Banana Barge."

"Who the devil made up those names?" asked Sid.

"My wife. She's a schoolteacher. Kind of a poet, too," said the soda jerk. "What flavors?"

Joyce looked up. "Chocolate," she said. "Butter pecan." She weighed each word, as if success or failure depended on her wise decision. "And . . . maple walnut."

"You got one more."

"Sid." She grasped his hand. "Please. Choose the fourth."

He tried to remember. "All right . . . I choose . . . cherry vanilla."

"Cherry vanilla," she repeated. "And cover it with marshmallow syrup."

The soda jerk tightened his white apron, and entered his laboratory. He lay out his instruments among the curved spigots, the contorted glass shapes, the mysterious creams and exotic syrups, the bubbling potions and sweet-smelling elixirs. He plunged his arm into a deep aluminum pit and pulled out a huge dip of bronze. "Butter pecan," he announced, a surgeon talking to a patient under local anesthesia.

"How does he know where they are?"

"Practice," she whispered. "It takes years of training." Was she kidding, just having fun? You never knew.

"Cherry vanilla. For the gentleman."

She watched every move, afraid he might leave something out, defraud her of a flavor, a dab of syrup, a fluff of whipped cream.

They towered like miniature gardens complete with ice-cream mountains, walnut boulders, whipped-capped peaks, deep fudge-filled rivers flowing inexorably to the banana plains below. Deftly, he moved the two barges from side to side, reverently filling them with the frozen, canned, machine-pressed, chemically-treated goodness of an American harvest . . .

The theatre was crowded. *The Redhot Redhead* had already started.

"That's Barbara Carol," said Joyce, pointing to a fifteen-foot henna giantess.

"C'mon baby," said Rob Gruff in a prissy voice. "How about a kiss."

"Why should I?" asked the Redhot Redhead.

" 'Cause. 'Cause I want to," he said, trying to make it a demand. Without waiting for an answer, he seized her, and, at the unseen bidding of Sam Le Vine, the director, she threw him to her bed, which a moment ago had been at the other end of the room, but which magically had moved closer, to provide a cozy nest for them to lay their eggs.

The next shot revealed the delicate pursuer beneath the Redhot Redhead's massive body, his eyes closed in ecstasy, his lips parted, his arms hanging limply over the sides, waiting for her to burst into flame.

The audience came to life. The Redhead began to finger Rob Gruff's tiny ears. The men in the audience pawed the country girls. The giantess ran her fingers through his curly locks; the men raked their stubby farm hands among the female hair roots. Then it came: the kiss.

But the girls were not as eager as the Redhot Redhead, whose salary had been computed at $3500 an embrace. Some allowed only a tiny, teasing peck. Others refused to obey the fifteen-foot mountain of breasts and thighs as she picked away at the Grecian body beneath her.

Suddenly the Legion of Decency stepped in. The Redhead dismounted. The men let go; the girls sat back, primly chewing their popcorn cud.

The celluloid unwound. Putting pieces together, Sid decided that the hero was a sex-criminal trying to go straight. Le Vine arranged to have Red's roommate, a masculine young woman in slacks, leave on a mysterious "errand." Once more the effeminate young man played at pursuit. Sid was confused.

Red's bed moved closer. She was on top again, red-hot and getting hotter. Off the sound track you could almost hear Le Vine's cursing: "For God's sake, some emotion, Gruff! Pretend she's a man!" This time the Redhead managed to sigh the sacred word—"marriage." The roommate reappeared as they revealed their newly hatched plans. Tearfully, she put her arms around the Redhot Redhead, congratulating the winner.

The next movie was all about love and death, war and vengeance, for which the producer had hired a succession of directors, the first, specializing in love, the next in death, the next in hate, the next in crime, till finally, dissatisfied, he concluded with the original, so that the picture began and ended with love.

At first a theme insinuated itself in small fragments, hints, dropped chords, pieces of motif. Levis Preem began to hum. A ninety-piece orchestra took up the tune of the Max Katz masterpiece which formed the film's title, *Hug Me Till I Die.*

Levis, unlike Gruff in the picture before, was a real he-man. Trouble was, he confused "lovin'" with "hatin'." He couldn't love without hatin'.

Then he joined the army and the audience discovered a second flaw in Levis' granite. He couldn't hate without lovin'. This was enough to earn him and the director who thought of the twist a dishonorable discharge. The first director was brought back.

A reunion. The ex-soldier sado-masochist surprised his sweetheart in her chintz-Limoges bedroom. "Come in," she said. He was already there, leering, in a bright new black-and-white undertaker's frock. She slipped into her chemise.

Now she, too, was dressed to kill. The rustling, the crunching grew dim. Levis sneaked into his song. The heroine took up the catchy limerick. The dubbed-in voices joined in a fiery duet; Levis Preem and his sweetheart opening and closing their mouths while sound specialists inserted the notes:

You can whip me, you can kick me,
You can throw me on the floor,

But Daddy, Daddy, Daddy,
Oh, I'll only love you more.

Yes I love you Daddy, Daddy,
Though you kissed me till I'm sore,

Though you beat me, though you squeeze me,
Oh, I'll only love you more.

Last night you almost choked me
And you called it just a kiss,

Now you're rippin' me to pieces—
Daddy, somethin's gone amiss.

But Daddy, don't stop, Daddy,
Even if I gotta cry,

Please Daddy, Oh my Daddy,
Just you hug me till I die.

Levis fastened his lips to her mouth, his hands circling her thin, scrawny neck. He meant business. Obediently the spectators followed suit. Undated girls howled with delight. Lone wolves hooted excitedly: "Kill her, man, kill her." The wolverines: "Love me, Levis, till I die."

[162]

Levis hugged and whacked, kissed and conked. The lone wolves howled for blood, and the lonesome girls yelled to be bled. The theatre grew darker; the exit lights blinked out. The chairs became racks, and love became a thing of hate. Inside a thousand, a hundred thousand bedrooms, in movie houses, parking lots, in barns, in cornfields, what was natural had become defiled and the defiled was now deified.

Sid jumped to his feet. "What a lousy movie!"

"Hey, mister, sit down."

Hate me love me, love me hate me, Daddy, Daddy . . .

"Please, Sid. Come back!"

The Tomahawk Bar and Grill. The juke box was so loud she had to shout. "Let's not have an argument. Not about something as silly as a couple of movies."

The music switched off. The mechanical arm searched for a new record. "I'm not arguing," he shouted, unaware of the sudden silence. People stared. Sid and Joyce looked at each other.

She crunched a pretzel. "Tomorrow it'll be all over."

"Can't we see each other in the fall?" he asked earnestly. She stirred her drink. "In Provincetown," he urged. "Mrs. Steiner's gonna set me up in business."

Joyce stuck her gum under the seat and took a drink.

"At least . . . I hope she will," said Sid. "It won't be anything fancy, but you can help me tend the shop."

She sighed heavily. "Let's dance, honey."

"But you haven't answered my question." Again that tune, an elaborate arrangement of something awfully familiar. His face pressed against her heavily rouged cheek. Their bodies rubbed, glided, dipped as they danced slowly, ignoring the frantic rhythm of the juke box. Gently, his lips touched hers. "I love you," he whispered. "I love you very much."

The crooner started to croak:

You can whip me, you can kick me.

Sid stopped, his lips pressed against hers, the dancers moving about, wildly now. "I love you," he whispered.

Though you kissed me till I'm sore.

He kissed her again, his tongue searching the warm hollow of her mouth.

"Break it up, buddy. This is a respectable place." The manager jabbed him in the back. They walked to their corner. The music was roaring. He looked into her eyes. His lips formed the words: "I love you. I love you."

He held her hand tighter, trying to root her to himself, to the small island of a table. The dance grew wilder. The dancers were rhythmically masturbating as if they were no longer in a bar, but among bushes, behind trees, their fists clenched, the sweat pouring down their cheeks like tears.

The music grew louder, smashing everything around them to bits. He gazed at her, surrounded by the rubble, the dirt, the ruins. She became more and more beautiful, like a flower trying to grow where it had once been fertile, where it was now barren, where self-expression no longer seemed possible, nor kindness, nor joy, nor love . . .

The music stopped. The dancers stood still. Someone tiptoed to the machine and gently dropped in a coin. Silently, they watched the steel arm hover over the black discs, stop, dip, pick it up, the hit, number one, the top tune, the winner:

Though you whip me, though you squeeze me,

"Gosh, let's get out of here," he shouted. "That song makes me sick."

Joyce grabbed her sunglasses and followed.

They were in her Cadillac. The headlights lit up a red, white and blue sign: CAMP OMONGO.

*Now you're rippin' me to pieces,
Daddy, somethin's . . .*

"Shut that damn thing off."

She turned off the radio. "Why are you in such a bad mood?"

"I'm not," he said petulantly. "Can't you get some classical music? You know how I feel about rock'n'roll."

"But that's the only thing they play around here. I asked you to stay just a minute or two and see the ending of a movie and you acted as if I was putting you through some awful ordeal."

"It *was* awful."

"Do you expect them to have first-run films up here in the woods?" She turned off the ignition. "Anyhow," she continued, "even if they were awful, it was fun being with you."

"It would have been more fun if we could have been some other place."

"Some other place? That's like saying it would have been more fun if I were some other age, younger, not a married woman about to get a divorce. Or if you were some other man, older maybe, rich, with a big career behind you."

"You're not old. And I'm not that young, either."

"I like you just as you are, Sid honey. I wouldn't want to change a thing. The last two days have been absolutely . . ." She groped for the right word. "Memorable."

"You make it sound like a funeral."

"Stop teasing. You know what I mean." He pulled her toward him. "Wait a minute," she said, getting rid of her gum.

"Are you happy with me?" he asked, putting his arms around her.

[165]

He watched her strangely innocent face as she lit a cigarette. "Baby, these past few days have been fascinating." She inhaled. The smoke worked like a drug, making her even younger, even more beautiful. She reached for the radio tuner. "Oh, I forgot." Like a child who'd almost been wicked, she looked at him, then placed her hand in his to keep it out of mischief. "How about you, haven't you been having a good time?" she asked.

Sid's freckled face grew passionate. "I'd like to give myself to you fully, every muscle and nerve in my body. I'd like to be with you forever. To make love to life," he vowed solemnly.

She was still breathing in her dark drug. "Make love to life," she repeated. "It all sounds . . . so young." Again she drew in the smoke.

Suddenly she stopped. She stared at him, surprised.

"What's the matter?"

She began to laugh, as if drunk. "That's why you're so crazy about me," she gasped, between giggles, "because I'm your first one."

"Oh, for gosh sakes," he said, flushing. "Cut it out." He grabbed hold of her, begging her to look at him, to stop laughing, to stop making believe he didn't exist, that he was just another one-night stand, not even a person, just an affair, something to forget, like a worn-out song. She was in a different world, a world filled with stale jokes and sly whispers. She couldn't stop. She'd been set in motion and the key thrown away. The laughter kept spilling out of her mechanized mouth.

"I'm sorry," she tried to say, the tears streaming from her dark eyes. She tried to stifle her laughter. "A virgin!" she screamed. "Cherry. Cherry vanilla."

He slammed the door.

"Please. Come back." He didn't look. "I want you."

He walked between the high trees, underneath the half

moon, alone. "Why? Why?" He was crying. Out loud. Trying to stop, to think of something else. She was so beautiful, so beautiful. Suddenly, as if he'd been punched in the groin, he doubled up at the side of the road. "Why?" he cried.

From the blackness: the sounds of birds, of insects; the sounds of foxes; wild sounds, quick sounds, sounds of pursuit, of capture; loving-mating sounds; howling-dying sounds; sounds of pain, of misery, of warning. "Why?" he sobbed. The sounds welled up from behind the trees, from the forest, from all the forests of the world, a crescendo of calls, rising to meet him, surrounding him, drowning him. But nowhere in all the noise and yells and whispers, nowhere was there an answer.

PURSUIT

JOYCE GREENBERG heard the bugle howling. It was a cry for help. Sid. She had to find him, to bring him back. The bugle, like a groan of dismay, her own stupidity, her selfishness, the notes trumpeting out, laughing at her diamond-covered body. If only she'd insisted on his driving back with her, insisted, the way she did with her husband. She ran frantically up and down between the rows of cabins, the bugle still blowing, the campers beginning to get up.

"A girl!"

"Duck! A woman!"

As if it mattered to her that they were naked and staring, crouching behind posts, jeering at her. As if anything mattered except finding him. "Sid," she cried, "Sid."

"Hey, Goldstein, your dick's showing."

"Sid."

"Goldy's got a hard on!"

"Come and get me," shouted Goldy. "I'm all yours, baby."

"Sid," she cried. "Where are you?"

"Fat Stuff, show her what you got."

"She'll never go for his. It's too small."

"Sid. Please."

"Get a load of Randy. He thinks that's a flag he's waving."

"Down from there, you guys. F' Christ's sake."

"Sid," she cried into the jungle of catcalls. "Come back."

"Didya hear that? She's callin' for Sid."

"Oh, Sid darling. Oh, Sid honey. Come to me, baby." They stretched out their naked arms in a mock, rapturous embrace. "Oh kiss me, Sid, kiss me, honey, I'm coming."

"Sid," she cried into the foul air, "where are you?"

"Here I am, your Sidsy Widsy. All hot and ready to go." They stood on their beds, hugging each other, fornicating on their white pillows.

"Cut it out," cried the bass voices, straining to catch a blurred glimpse of her legs, her breasts.

"Look at Gans. He got the biggest one here!"

"Where'd she come from?"

"From heaven, boy. Straight from . . ."

"Sid. Where are you?"

"He's not here, and you shouldn't be here either, Mrs. Greenberg." A harsh, raspy, bitter voice. Sylvia Steiner's.

"Where is he?" she demanded.

[168]

"They're all looking," cried Mrs. Steiner. "Are you out of your head?"

They stopped in front of Steiner's colonial house.

"Please. Won't you tell me," begged Mrs. Greenberg. "Where is he?"

"Do you realize you've upset the whole camp," shouted Sylvia. "We'll never hear the end of this."

"Tell me where he is," cried Joyce. "I need him."

Mrs. Steiner clung to the wooden railing, as if it were a spar, as if she'd been shipwrecked, as if she were just about to go under. "Damn you, I know all about it. Sure he's good-looking, that doesn't mean you run screaming through the camp!"

"I want him back." She grabbed hold of Sylvia's paint-stained smock.

Mrs. Steiner picked off the hand, a disgusting insect. The bugle blew again. "Slut!" she shouted.

The campers were lining up. The fluted door with the brass knocker slowly opened. The Great White Father stepped out. "Good morning, ladies."

"Where is he?" she cried. "Tell me."

"Lovely morning. I heard you chatting, Mrs. Greenberg. Thought I'd come down and say hello. Thought maybe you'd forgotten all about that promise you made to see me after the banquet, so we could have a little talk."

"She didn't forget," cried Mrs. Steiner. "You damn fool!"

"Now, Sylvia. Please!" Trying to retain his composure, to smile. "Mrs. Greenberg—now, Sylvia, will you shut up— Mrs. Greenberg, I want you to know what a pleasure it's been to have your son . . . ." He paused. "Your son . . . ." The name wouldn't come. Of all times! Randy? No, that was the other one. The poor one. Berney? That was the fat one.

[169]

"Norman! For God's sakes, don't you even know?" shouted Sylvia. "Norman Greenberg."

"Of course," said the Great White Father, stepping over the obstacle. "A wonderful camper, Mrs. Greenberg. I'll eat my hat if that boy doesn't win the Most Improved Intermediate Award. I wish you and your husband could . . ."

He'd tripped again! Quickly he rose to his knees. "I only wish you, Mrs. Greenberg, you, his mother, could have been here to . . ."

"Where is he?"

"Lining up for breakfast with the other Intermediates."

"You fool!" cried Mrs. Steiner. "She doesn't mean her son. She means Tannenbaum."

His smile evaporated.

"Don't you know what's going on?" shouted Sylvia. "They've been sleeping together," she cried. She turned to Joyce. "Well, you can't have him. I sent him away. He won't be back till you're gone."

"Sylvia!" whined the Great White Father.

The loudspeaker was thumping out a spirited march. The campers, in close-drill formation, proceeded to the Parade Grounds.

"I suppose I should have tried to make our lovely visitor happy. I suppose I should have encouraged all our strong, handsome counselors to make love to her. What are you trying to do, turn Omongo into a whore house?"

The two hundred campers lined up like robots in front of the flagpole.

"Mrs. Greenberg," shouted Steiner. She was running to the parking ground. The Great White Father ran after her. The robots laughed.

She had to find him. She flicked the ignition key. If only it wasn't too late.

[170]

"Come back," he shouted. "The camp!" His whole world collapsing as the Cadillac got smaller, as the bankbook slid out of reach.

Norman watched the black dot, like the end of a sentence: stop, finished. Without a single good-bye!

DEPARTURE

"WHERE'VE YOU BEEN?" asked Mrs. Levine, angrily.

Mr. Levine looked at his watch. "We shouldn't have waited."

"We'll make it," she said. "Mr. Whatshisname, Mr. Hawk, said he'll take us to the station."

"You ready?" said Eagle, his elbow resting against the open window.

"We still have over an hour to meet the bus. From here, it only takes fifteen minutes."

"Might be twenty," said Eagle.

She turned to Randy. "Plenty of fresh vegetables," she was saying, "nap every day, rubbers when it rains, every day write . . ."

"Get plenty of them medals," shouted Mr. Oronsky, patting Mike on the back as they leaned against their brand-new Buick. "Especially swimming. We don't have any of those."

Mr. and Mrs. Kahn stood beside their conservative two-year-old Chevrolet. "Do your best, Mel," Mr. Kahn was

[171]

saying. "That's all we expect. You can't be first in everything."

Mr. and Mrs. Halpern sat in their Chrysler Imperial
Convertible with the top down. "Now, Berney, try not to
eat too much," his father was saying. "We want you to be
well, when you come home. There's a lot of studying ahead
of you, son."

"B. Halpern—Surgeon," said his mother, smiling.

"A doctor has to study hard. Right, pal?"

"Straight A," said Fat Stuff. "The best."

Cars started leaving. Stout arms waved monogrammed
handkerchiefs from the sedan windows.

"Plenty of orange juice," his mother was saying. "Your
father's employer distinctly told me you could get all the
fresh orange juice you wanted if only you made sure to
ask."

"You got to make yourself heard in this world," said
Mr. Levine. "If you don't speak up . . ."

"Pop."

"Your father's talking. What do you interrupt him
for?"

"It's important," said Randy. "I got something to ask."

"What's on your mind?" said Mr. Levine, glad to be
called on for advice.

"It's private, Dad. I got to talk to you in private." His
father looked bewildered. He was no longer smiling. He put
his hands in his pockets. He fumbled with his change.

"Your father don't keep anything from me," said his
mother, angrily. "And I don't expect *you* to keep anything
from me, either."

"I got to talk to him. Alone."

"Nothing doing," she shouted. "If it's so important, you
can let me in on it, too."

"It's about Mr. Oronsky. It's . . ."

"Esther, hurry, we'll be late. We'll miss our bus."

"It'll only take a minute, Dad."

"We can't keep Mr. Hawk waiting forever," begged his father. "His time's valuable. He's getting paid for it. Overtime."

"So what's the big secret?" asked his mother, smiling.

"It's about Pop's boss. How he got me to come here." She froze, as if she suddenly remembered something.

"The bus," shouted Mr. Levine.

"I got to find out. Mike says . . ."

"Never mind the Oronsky boy," she whispered angrily. "A spoiled child, that's all he is."

"Is it true?" demanded Randy, pulling his mother by her sleeve.

"I don't know what you're talking about," she cried. "And I don't want to know. Your father works and slaves so you can become a success. Then you accuse him of being a liar."

"I didn't say that!"

"I'm telling you, it doesn't pay to have children."

"Kiss him, Esther. Make up. Say good-bye."

"Your father's the most honest man there is," cried Mrs. Levine.

"The union!" shouted Randy. "What about . . ."

His mother smothered him with a great big kiss. His father grabbed his hand. "Good-bye," they shrieked in unison.

Eagle stepped on the gas. The station wagon roared away.

PREPARATIONS FOR WAR

THE SCHEDULE and its carefully planned hatreds could be resumed, as if the parents with their innocent meddling had never been there. The mothers and fathers had returned to their strange planet, remembering Omongo simply as a playground, a vacation spot. Now that they were gone, the contests grew bitter again.

The war. Everyone talked about it. Was it true the awards had already arrived, at midnight, in a heavy steel car, with the Great White Father himself, surrounded by an armed guard, placing the precious package in the camp safe? Was it true the final event would be a treasure hunt with the Great White Father and Flinn, like pirates, right now plotting X's on a mysterious map, burying secret clues while everyone was asleep?

And then—the cup. Tier upon tier, two feet high, surrounded by gold-plated runners, wrestlers, tennis stars, baseball champs, America's Sporting Saints, and above them, a wide uncarved surface for the name of the winner.

The winner of the cup was a person apart. There was no award for second, not in the war. It was first or nothing. Win or lose.

One morning at flag-raising, the announcement: Gans, leader of the Blues! Leader of the Reds, Lieutenant Flinn! Cheers, catcalls. From then on Gans and Flinn walked around like heroes, avoiding each other. The war grew closer.

Intrigues. Some were for Gans, a champ himself, who'd even won the cup. They'd sneak into his tent at night and stick secret notes under his pillow, selling themselves, what terrific athletes they were, what great assets they'd be if only he'd take them on, if only he'd fix it.

Lieutenant Flinn was courted, too. With dollar bills and scribbles begging him to accept them.

The teams fought harder, as if the war had already broken out. To lose even a single inning was an omen of defeat. Winning was a prediction of victory. The Great White Father spent every day planning, plotting, smoothing out details. Just over the horizon, the war drifted closer, like an ominous, mushrooming cloud.

It was only a matter of time.

"Ready," shouted Mel.

Mike put out his arms in a V for Victory.

Randy was set, his knees slightly bent.

"Go!"

They jumped. Everyone leaned over to see whose dive was longest.

Fat Stuff looked puzzled. "Levine's ahead," he yelled, trying to figure out who was who.

Randy let go with everything he had, the water splitting, giving way like the Red Sea, as if it were afraid. His hand slapped the pier. The cheering stopped.

Fat Stuff ran up. "Atta boy, Levine!"

Mel cupped his hands to his mouth. "The winner, by a head," he shouted, "Mike Oronsky."

Fat Stuff stopped smiling. "Rigged!" he cried.

"You keep the . . . hell . . . out of this," muttered Mike, out of breath, as he leaned against Kahn, his buddy, his pimp.

Fat Stuff stepped back. It wasn't worth getting slugged just for a swimming race.

"I was first," shouted Randy.

"Yeah," said Mel, "you were the first one up the ladder. But he was the first one to win."

"It was all fixed between you and Mel," cried Randy.

"How the hell do you know?" said Mel. "You can't tell what's happening when you're swimming."

"I could hear him behind me," shouted Randy. "A couple of feet."

"So now the wise-guy claims he measured it," cried Mike. "What do you, carry a ruler with you?"

"Yeah," cried Goldstein. "His cock. It measures two inches. Only he thinks it's two feet."

"The judge is a crook," said Randy. "A stool pigeon."

"Crook!" shouted Mike. "The only reason you're here is because your old man's a crook. And you're not as innocent as you been trying to make out."

"I don't know what you're talking about," cried Randy. But he did. He knew now. That cheat! "Take that back about my old man, God damn it, or I'll shove it back."

"You and what army," sneered Mike.

"Me and my bare fists," cried Randy.

"Oh boy," said Fat Stuff, "a fight."

"Listen, jerks, you get your knuckles all cut up, they'll keep you out of the war," warned Mel.

"I'll wrestle him then," shouted Randy.

Fat Stuff pulled out a bankroll. "Make your bets now, before the fighting begins." He flipped the bills like a pack of cards.

"You got to give us odds," said Goldstein. "We're not going to put our money on Levine just 'cause he won the race."

"That's right!" cried Randy. "I won and you guys know it."

"Put up or shut up," said Fat Stuff.

"Hey, Mel. What's the matter?" whispered Mike. "Where's your dough—lose your confidence?"

"Hell, Mike, no. It's just that, well . . . O.K.," he shouted. "I'm putting two bucks down on Mike here."

"Come on you guys. Let's see some action. We ain't got all night."

"Yeah, who's afraid of who?" yelled Fat Stuff. "Who's the guy who's yellow?"

They kept on turning, stalking, feinting, then retreating, as if now that they were in the ring, they no longer wanted to fight, as if their hate had turned to suspicion, as if their suspicion was changing to fear.

"Even TV's better than this," groaned Goldstein.

"Let's put our money in a bank. We'll collect interest."

In a flash, they were at each other, grabbing, pulling, punching.

Mike had him by the ankles. He was down on top. Then it was Randy, rolling over, his hands gripping Mike's neck.

"Thata boy," cried the investors. "You show him."

"Come on, Mike. I got my dough on you," shouted Fat Stuff.

Mike's knees were free. He started jamming them into Randy's back.

"Hold on, Levine, hold on."

Now Mike was on top, punching, whamming. Randy's face twisted. He swung his arms free. "Get him! Get him!" With a single wallop, he landed a hard one, right in Mike's belly. Fat Stuff groaned.

"Thata boy," shouted Goldy.

Now Randy was on top, jamming down with his knees, slugging away. Mike's right eye ballooned. Randy ground his knee into Oronsky's stomach. Mike grunted as the air got knocked out of him, a soft sound, like a quiet cheer.

[177]

"Over, Mike. Turn him over."

Then Randy really let him have it. He shoved his fist into Mike's crotch.

"Ouch," cried Fat Stuff. "I felt that one myself."

"Thata boy, Randy. That's placing 'em."

"Mike! Mike!" cried Mel, on his knees, following every punch. "F' Christ sake, get up! I got all my money on you." Mike groaned in pain, whispering *oo, oo,* again and again as fists, knees, elbows rained down on him.

"Just hold out till he gets tired," advised Fat Stuff.

Randy grabbed Mike's arm and twisted it like a corkscrew. "Say Uncle!" he roared.

Mike muttered. It wasn't Uncle. Randy twisted harder.

"You'll break it."

Mike's bruised face squirmed.

"Uncle?" demanded Randy. "Uncle?"

Snap! Like a branch.

"Jesus!"

They pulled back.

"You broke it."

"Uncle!" whimpered Mike.

Goldstein grabbed his winnings and ran.

"Let's get the hell away from here."

Everything would work out. Mike would come crawling back. He'd wash the blood off and everything would be all right again. Maybe he was on his way back now. Randy climbed into the sagging bed. Norman's sack was still empty. Cohen was out too, drinking probably.

What if Mike was really hurt? What if he told his father and Mr. Oronsky fired him? His mother would wallop the daylights out of him, that's what! She'd hit him till he was black and blue. She'd drag him to Mr. Oronsky and make him apologize. To Mike, too.

"Out of bed, you!" The bright beam stabbed his eyes.

[178]

It was Cohen. Hopping mad. "What do you guys know about it?"

Randy and Mel looked at each other.

"Listen, if you kids co-operate, you got nothing to worry about. First of all, Oronsky hasn't said a thing."

"Mike?" Randy looked up. "Is something wrong with him?"

"You want to get a smack in the kisser?" shouted Cohen. "The poor jerk was screaming loud enough to wake up the dead. The nurse thinks it's a broken arm."

"You mean he won't be in the war?" Randy smiled.

"That's right, he won't be in the war. The main thing now is to get it healed before the season's over, so his old man won't find out. Right now, even the Great White Father doesn't know. Before we tell him, we got to get together on a good story. I'm on your side."

"So you're on our side," said Randy. "Sure, and we know why. Because you're responsible. Because you're the counselor. So don't get buddy-buddy with us."

Cohen took out a cigarette. He put it back. "Look," he said. "This is it: we were all down on the pier, getting in shape for the war. Oronsky tripped and fell. When we went to pick him up, we found he had a broken arm."

They nodded.

"And when your pal Greenberg comes traipsing in . . ."

"He's no pal of mine," said Randy. "All he cares about now is making mud pies with Pansybaum."

"You should have beat that Greenberg guy up, too," said Mel.

"You mean it was Levine?" Cohen started to laugh. "How'd you do it?"

"We were all down on the pier practicing for the war."

"The truth," demanded Cohen.

"That's it." Randy winked.

"Stop lying."

"You want an investigation?" smiled Randy. "We're all honest around here, see. Even Mike. Unless he starts blabbing. Then *he'll* be the liar, not us. So save your name-calling. Save it in case Oronsky starts to squeal."

Mel clamped his hands over his mouth to stop laughing. He buried his head under the pillow. What a character, that Levine. What cold nerve. What a guy; a great guy; what a champ . . .

Steiner looked at the War Schedule, a large chart with squares and arrows: team against team; winner vs. winner; and at the bottom, clear across the chart, a space marked TREASURE HUNT.

Omongo would be saved. He'd show her the colored movies. He'd explain to Mrs. Greenberg how much Omongo meant to these boys, what a great training it was for later life. No, too fancy. He'd make it personal. He'd promise to name the Social Hall after her. The Joyce Greenberg Memorial. No, the Joyce Greenberg Hall, that was more like it. When she died he would . . . Better not mention that.

Flinn marched in, all nuts and bolts. His face was grim. A red sash was wrapped around his chest.

"Sit down, Lieutenant," Steiner shouted lustily. "How does it feel to be leader of the Red Tribe?"

"It's an honor," spouted Flinn. "And I know we're going to win, sir."

Steiner lit a cigarette. "Lieutenant, have you been wondering why I picked you, a new counselor, as leader of half the camp?"

Flinn looked modest. He knew it was something inside him, something which Steiner instinctively recognized. He fingered his red sash.

The Great White Father cleared his throat. "Because, well, my wife . . . What's the matter?"

Flinn was pale. "I knocked it over, sir. I'll pick it up."

[180]

Steiner looked at the broken glass. "Forget it. We're all on edge. Battle nerves."

Flinn tried piecing the ashtray together. His hands were trembling.

"My wife thinks I should bring in more counselors like you, who've taken American names, who are trying to fit in."

"I had to," shouted Flinn. "Flinklestein! They'd never make me an officer."

"Don't apologize. We need more like you, Flinn. Gentiles, too, like Preston."

"Those kids got to learn," said Flinn, wiping the sweat from his forehead. "In this world it don't pay to be so damn different."

"You know the score," said the Great White Father, rising to his feet. "I want the campers to know, too. So when they get out there, in life, they'll be ready with drawn knives, confident, eager to win, to stab. Because that's what life is. Life is war, a bloody murderous war. And do you want to know something?" He drew close as if to whisper something unbelievably obscene: "That's why I like it."

STEINER'S TEN

▐▐▐

I. Thou shalt have no other loyalties before me for I am the Lord Steiner who hath led thee from bondage in the land of thy parents.

II. All graven images shall be as follows: Gold for first; Silver for second; Bronze for third; and Strontium 90 for the rest.

III. Thou shalt not take the name of the Great White Father, thy leader, to be vain.

IV. On the Sabbath, follow the schedule.

V. Show honor to thy parents, who pay,
But it's the Great White Dad you obey.

VI. Thou shalt kill for God and country on demand.

VII. Thou shalt adulterate the water, pollute the land, and poison the air for the sake of our fathers' pride.

VIII. Thou shalt steal only if thou canst prove thyself innocent.

IX. Thou shalt witness falseness and smile.

X. Thou shalt not covet thy neighbor's house, nor his wife, nor his auto, but a bigger, better, newer . . .

The Great White Father arose. What a nightmare. He looked at his chronometer. Was he crazy napping like this the night of the war!

Frenetic murmurs drowned the camp. The insects' scratching, the birds' cawing seemed more frantic, as if nature too were in on this, not as spectator, but as warrior.

The drums had come to the end of the record. The *swunsh, swunsh* of the needle reverberated throughout the camp. He grabbed the arm and put it back at the beginning. He turned the speed, the volume, the tone, faster, louder, deeper.

ON THE BRINK

SLOWLY, HYPNOTICALLY, the drums throbbed through the loudspeaker.

"Aren't you ready yet?" shouted Cohen. "I can't leave till I check you out."

"What about Greenberg?" Mel spread out his clothes.

"All right," muttered Cohen, "so there's a rotten apple in the barrel. What do you want me to do?"

Cohen looked at Levine, stacking underwear, rolling socks into small, efficient puffs. What an improvement. You wouldn't know it was the same guy, who only six weeks ago was fumbling around, asking crazy questions, looking stupid. Like the poem he used to recite in school about the Statue of Liberty and the ignorant greenhorns who first came and what the statue thought when it saw them gawking. *Give me your stupid masses yearning to be rich, the human garbage of your teeming slums.* Something like that. Only now it wasn't the statue talking. It was a huge Omongo Indian and he was roaring, with a shrill, bugle voice: "Give us your lost, your scared, your Momma's babies, your hunched-up bookworms. And we'll make them winners, champs, Americans." There was something about Omongo that changed a guy forever. He knew. It had happened to him.

"Hurry," said Cohen. "The drums'll stop soon. You know what that means."

"The war!" cheered Mel, standing on his bed.

"You bet," said Cohen.

"On my mark," cried Mel. "Ready set go, go, go for the Reds, Reds, Reds!"

"Cool off," said Randy. A bunch of hotheads. He shoved his clothes to one side, making a special place. Reserved. Next time he opened the lid would be to put it away, in that empty space: what he'd fought for; what he'd won. With his own two hands he'd place it there, in his dad's cheap, two-bit, battered trunk—the gold cup.

SICK BAY

NORMAN STEPPED BACK to get a better look. Over a foot high. Sid had been afraid it wouldn't work.

"What's your rush?" asked Tannenbaum. "If you don't finish now, you can do it later. The world won't end just because there's going to be a war."

Norman turned his back. It had to be right. He thought of his white clay cup, dug up after thousands of years, piece by piece, cemented together, the museum man standing back, just the way *he* was doing now, judging it, thinking it was pretty damn good. The museum man squinting. A flaw! It would be there forever, in the museum, wrong forever. He smoothed it out.

A soft knocking. The drums. No, the door. What if Steiner found him? They were supposed to be in their tents getting ready, talking it up, the war, the war, that goddam war . . .

Sid motioned him to get back. "Who's there?" he shouted.

"It's me, Sylvia." She was drunk. Her voice blurred the brittle words. "I have to see you." The door shook as she pounded against it, singing, serenading him. "Whip me, kick me, toss me on a floor. Daddy, Daddy, Daddy, I'll just love you up some more." She held the last note in her quivering voice.

"Sid baby. Love you." She hammered the words on the door. "Need you. I'll die if you don't open."

"You're already dead," he shouted. "Go away." He turned to Norman. "You better leave, fella. Before there's trouble."

"So damn it, screw her if you wanta," said Norman. "Just let me finish my cup."

"Leave it here," said Sid, embarrassed. "I'll put it in the kiln myself."

Norm ran to the door. "Tonight," he yelled. "Do it tonight."

The Great White Father turned the knob. The recording wheeled around faster. Fantastic idea of his. An inspiration. From that play. About a man who went out to conquer a jungle. All the time, those drums. At first they were so soft you hardly knew they were there. Then louder and faster, until you were right up at the edge of your chair, your heart beating a mile a minute. A great way to work up excitement.

Eagle thought he heard something. How could you tell? What sounded like a howl might be a little bird. What sounded like wind cutting through the leaves might be a whole tribe, the Omongo Indians, clutching their daggers, advancing.

The drums. Steiner was always adding something new.

They sounded like the war drums of his own people crawl-ing behind the trees, thousands of them, coming back to kill the Jews.

Would he join them, he the dead, stuffed Eagle? Would he throw away his whiskey bottle, rip off his clothes, put on the war paint? The drums roared. His blood grew hot, as if an old fire had been rekindled.

"Hey, you down there," shouted Mike.

Eagle looked up.

"What the hell are those drums for?"

"War drums, little boy. The Omongos in the forest. They're coming back."

"You ignorant loony, that's from the loud speaker. Damn, why did it have to happen to me? I'd give up my whole arm if I could be there."

Someone coming! From the woods. She raced around the corner of the infirmary, as if the Indians were after her powdered scalp. "Evening, Mrs. Steiner," he bowed. She didn't even notice. He spit on the ground.

Those drums. Flinn felt like strangling, mangling, rip-ping. Like winning. Like the good old days in the gym, with the smell of stale sweat, among those horses, pinions, wheels, a chamber of torture, the groans, getting up, stumbling; arms, legs, on top, on bottom; turning over and over, his skin, wet, hot, slippery; rubbing against the wrestler's naked body, igniting finally, like a match. A fight made all the other times, the in-between times at his desk, not life at all, but purgatory, waiting for a war.

"Who's that!"

"It's me. Sylvia." She was out of breath.

"What do you want?"

"Tannenbaum. He's going to tell my husband that you lied to him, that you're really not Jewish at all, that you just said it to get the job."

He stepped back. Her face was wrinkled like a dried red leaf. "You're drunk!" he cried.

The drums stopped. There was a stillness, the silence of a tomb. The animals and the insects and the owls and the campers were suddenly hushed, as if they were all parts of the huge machine. The yellow moon, like an altar candle, flickered nervously in the sky. Even the wind stopped. The warm air lay trapped beneath the ground. Steiner moved his finger. Silence. Complete. Perfect. The silence of death.

"Damn him!" cried Sylvia. "Why couldn't he wait?"

Flinn gravely lifted his knapsack to his shoulders and marched toward the Parade Grounds. "The war," he muttered. "It's begun."

JUBAGO

RABBI YESLIN walked through the fiery opening. Solemnly, he draped the Sears Roebuck blanket around his shoulders. "Ladies and gentlemen."

Screams of laughter. "Ladies! Let me at 'em."

"Gentlemen. Yoo hoo, gentlemen."

The old rabbi was laughing, too. They were with him, in a good mood. If only they would turn down the campfire. Impressive, very impressive, but a little too hot.

"Whatever side you are on, God is on that side also."

Applause for God. His benedictions should only make such enthusiasm in Brooklyn. The fire detail rushed to feed the flames. "War," continued the rabbi, "a part of life."

"War," they cried. "War. We want more."

The yelling grew louder. Yeslin turned to the congregation. What spirit. Instead of the sleepy muttering he was used to. All this time he'd misjudged.

"*Boruch shem k'vod . . .*" The campers were getting restless. *Malchuso l'olom v'oed.*" He was losing them. He cast away his libretto. With a flourish, he reached under his blanket and pulled out the sacred ram's horn. That would get them.

It did. The chorus began again. "Yipee for Yez. Three cheers!" This was better than a bar mitzvah. Back and forth he swayed, as if the ram's horn had turned into a jazz trumpet. He was a hit. He'd crashed through the walls of their indifference.

Eagle, in a headpiece of bright feathers and a rawhide cowboy suit, two toy pistols strapped around his waist, staggered up the platform.

"A real Indian!" cried the Midgets.

"Drunk," shouted the older campers.

"With a tomahawk."

"That's just an old hammer."

Eagle looked at them through the flames. Steiner had told him to talk in Indian. What did he know? He'd never even heard it except when he was a boy. Maybe not even then.

"Godumkikgidout."

"Look! He's talking Indian."

"Kikgidout," they repeated.

"Jubastedgo!"

"Jubago!" they cried. "Jubago!"

As if it were part of the ancient Indian ritual, the campers kneeled, kissing the earth. "Dance," they shouted. "We wanta see a war dance."

Eagle ripped off his feathered cap and threw it into the flames. He pulled out his toy revolvers and shot, bullet after bullet after bullet, until they were all dead, then stumbled to the ground.

"Get him out of here," commanded Preston. "He's drunk."

The station wagon roared up to third base. The chanting stopped.

"The Great White Father!"

Steiner walked ponderously, ceremoniously, toward the roaring flames. The loudspeaker tuned in on "The Star-Spangled Banner." Everyone snapped to attention. The Great White Father was wearing a red and blue robe. And in his hands, gleaming in the firelight, three feet high at least, was the cup!

Then conquer we must . . . Randy's knees trembled. The music soared. The Great White Father, a zombie, marched toward him, the cup high over his head. Randy put out his arm, way out, and with the tips of his fingers, just as the cup passed, he touched it.

The campers were pale. You could see tears around their eyes. *In triumph shall wave* . . . It was so great, Randy had to turn away to keep from crying himself.

"Fellow Tribesmen of Omongo."

Applause. Calls for quiet.

"We are met on the great battlefield of our war for the first time, testing whether this institution, or any institution conceived and dedicated to the noble spirit of America, can long endure."

Cheers. An announcement.

"This year, the cup will be awarded to the winner of the treasure hunt."

More applause.

"Fellow Tribesmen," his voice grew solemn. "Our war will begin at dawn. Tonight you'll all join in singing. The Red Tribe on one side, the Blues on the other. And then

you'll sleep and wait for the sun to rise, as soldiers all over
the world are waiting, in trenches, in battlefields, in ships,
watching and praying, now, for the battle to begin. It is
altogether fitting and proper that we should do this. For we
here highly resolve that the glorious spirit of Omongo shall
not perish from the earth."

All hell broke loose. The Great White Father de-
scended from the altar. They lifted him. Steiner arose and
like the Statue of Liberty holding out the torch, with one
mighty thrust of his arm he held aloft the cup, beckoning
them to follow him to glory.

FORAY

"I'M NOT KIDDING," said Flinn.

Cohen threw another log into the fire. "Why should he
do a thing like that?"

"He's nuts," said Flinn. "He's a misfit here and he hates
us for it. Why do you think Steiner kept him out of this
war? Because he don't want him to louse things up."

"And that's why Steiner'll never believe him," smiled
Cohen. "No matter how he lies."

"What if he tells the old man we've been screwing
around with some of the girls in town."

Cohen stopped laughing. "How does he know?"

Flinn shrugged. "From old Eagle eyes. What's it matter? Anyhow, Tannenbaum knows. Mrs. Steiner told me.
He'll kick us out on our ears."

"F' Christ's sake," cried Cohen, "let's not get upset about a queer like Tannenbaum. We'll take care of him tomorrow."

A voice. Cohen jumped back.

"It's me, Gans." He was wearing a long blue sash over his sweatshirt. "I want to find out if there's points for the team that wins the treasure hunt."

"No points," said Cohen, "but the old man's going to let the winning captain present the cup."

"Big deal," sneered Gans, strutting off as if he'd already won the war.

Flinn turned to Cohen. "Don't forget," he whispered. "Tomorrow. Tannenbaum."

"I'm with you," said Cohen.

Flinn walked back.

"Hey, Lieutenant, what's up?" asked one of the Seniors.

Flinn mounted the box. "Listen," he shouted, "I don't say this is definite, but there's a strong, strong smell coming from out there." He pointed toward the Blues. "The Captain of the Blues has been trying to make a fix."

"With the judges?"

"Yeah," shouted Flinn. "Now, Cohen and the other referees are honest, so you don't have to worry. Only I want you to know they've been approached."

Mutters. Threats.

"O.K.," grinned Flinn. "So you're mad. What are you red-blooded Reds going to do about it?"

He looked down. They were gone, running, charging through no-man's land, past Cohen and Preston and Epstein.

"The Reds!"

"Help!"

"The food," cried Fat Stuff. "They got the food!"

They threw cans and trampled loaves. Ketchup poured like blood across the battlefield. Three Blue counselors captured a squirming Red. They hoisted him up and carried him toward the flames.

The Reds were surrounded, pushed back, knocked down. They began to retreat, sliding over the baloney, rolling across the hot dogs, stumbling among the potato chips.

Flinn was waiting. "That's the spirit," he cheered. "We're going to win."

"They got, they got . . ." Randy tried to catch his breath. ". . . a prisoner."

"One of our men?"

"Yeah," cried Randy. "Kahn. Mel Kahn."

"That's the end of him," groaned Goldstein.

A scream, loud and murderous, from the enemy camp.

THE DAWN'S EARLY LIGHT

RUNNING, RUNNING, they were running, everyone, in the moonlight; everyone, running after it. It was getting brighter, blazing, sputtering, a ball of incandescent yellow. Randy reached out; so hot, his hands were melting, his flesh flowing into the red hot, gold hot, gold, gold cup, the blinding cup . . .

"Wake up!"

The rising sun, a ball of gold.

"Wake up," repeated Flinn, prodding them with his feet. "This is it," he shouted. "The war."

A long sword-shaped cloud stabbed into the sun. The bright, burning gold disappeared. Randy blinked his eyes. He reached out from his sleeping bag, as far as he could. The cup was gone.

THE JOUSTERS

PRESTON BLEW HIS WHISTLE. The horsemen crouched. The grapplers climbed up on their shoulders, as the ones underneath slowly rose, buckling under the weight, finally standing. It was the horse's game to jockey around, to find an opening, to charge, catch another team, a horse and his mount, by surprise. Then the grapplers would fight it out, trying to haul each other down, to win, to go on to the next attack. At the end of ten minutes the score would be taken. Every horse still with his rider would win a whole point for his tribe.

Where was Mel? It had all been set the day before. Kahn was to be the horse. Randy would ride him.

On top of someone else! A Senior, a goddam Senior! Randy turned away. That prisoner of war crap. Kahn was their hero now. *Remember Mel.* That was their motto.

Greenberg. "C'mon," yelled Randy. "Hurry up or we'll be disqualified."

Norman shrugged. "Don't do me any of your big favors, Levine."

"I got no choice." Quickly he pushed Norman down.

He mounted. Preston blew his whistle again. The battle was on.

They began to advance, a step at a time, the grapplers stretching out their arms like giant pincers, their fingers like claws, their mouths snapping insults, threats.

"Don't listen!" cried Randy. "They just look bigger than us. Don't let 'em get you excited."

Norman plodded toward the Blues. In the center of the field, half a dozen teams had already been knocked out, their grapplers pulled to the ground.

"Don't get nervous," whispered Randy. "Move toward the left. That's it, pal. There's a guy coming. Stand your ground. Brace yourself. Feet apart, damn it. Here they come!"

Randy reached out. He grabbed a Blue, the smallest Midget he could find. But the Blue horse was shrewd. He kept moving, matching Greenberg step for step, advancing as if the kid was a unicorn's horn cemented into him. Nothing, nothing could pull it out.

Randy began to twist the kid's arm.

"No fair," squeaked the brat.

The hell. No rule said you couldn't. Anyhow, the judges were somewhere else.

The kid tumbled to the ground. He'd won their first battle. "Nice going," said Randy, suddenly remembering the jerk who was carrying him. "Just keep it up," he grinned, patting him on the back as if he was a horse, a real one.

A pair of arms gripped him around the waist, tightening its coil like a hungry cobra.

"They got me!" he cried. "Turn! Turn!"

Inch by inch, Norman managed to twist around. Finally Randy faced the snake. Fat Stuff Halpern! Randy cocked his arm and let it fly into his belly. With a groan, Fat Stuff fell, pulling his Senior horseman with him. Randy laughed.

Off balance! Falling forward. Norman tried to pull him back onto his shoulders. Too late.

He looked at the Reds and Blues, tumbling all around him like bowling pins. Randy scrambled to his feet. "Get down," he whispered to Norman. "Hurry. Before they see us."

"But we're out," said Norman.

"You're not out till the judges see you, dope. Bend over. Before a referee looks this way."

"I see what you're trying to do," cried Cohen. "Back to the sidelines and make it snappy, Levine."

Randy threw a stone. "Damn it," he cried. "And we could have won, too!"

Norman wanted to tell him to go to hell, but Randy walked away. How could he explain it was just a game set up by that gray-haired bastard sitting in that rocking chair of his. Why did guys like Randy all take this kid stuff so serious?

MARINE COMBAT

RANDY SWAM ONE WAY, then the other, searching, panting for breath. There it was, the large white ball in front of him. One of the Blues had thrown it too far. They were hunting for it themselves, frantically, slapping the water with their arms as if they were beating the bushes for an escaped convict.

He swam toward it. Slowly, so they wouldn't notice. He'd trick them.

Someone else had it! Swimming with it, full speed, toward the goal. Greenberg! "Pass it," shouted Randy.

The others were looking the wrong way, at Kahn, faking, at the other end, shouting that he had it, splashing around so they wouldn't know what was going on.

Greenberg was almost at the line. He'd score. The Blue goalie wasn't even around. Damn it. Greenberg would get all the credit, a lousy swimmer like that, a guy who didn't even care.

"Pass it! Pass it!" The goal was right ahead. One flick of his wrist and he could have scored it himself, right now. Randy dove under. He could see Norman's skinny legs kicking around, clumsy, like a cripple. He grabbed them and pulled him down.

Randy gave a yank. Greenberg held on, his fingers digging into the ball as if it were a piece of sticky clay, as if he couldn't let go, even if he tried, as if it had hardened around his fingers. He jammed his elbow into Norm's belly. He wouldn't even open his eyes to see what was going on, to see that it wasn't an enemy who was punching him, but a teammate, a friend, Randy.

"There it is!"

"Get him."

The Reds were cheering, as Randy headed for the goal with the ball. Greenberg's exhausted face floated to the surface like a piece of garbage. The toss. The whistle. Perfect!

"Too late," the Blues shouted. "Game's over."

"Too late your ass," cried Randy. "I threw it before the whistle."

Cohen blew his whistle again. "The Blues," he announced, "three to two."

[196]

Even if he'd scored, it would have been a tie. The hell with it. Greenberg, that son-of-a-bitch.

Randy jerked off his bathing suit. The Blues were still out on the pier, whooping it up. They were coming into the locker room now, in bunches, like monkeys, as if the medals were bananas, as if they'd just been fed.

"Tomorrow morning, I'll be wearing that bronze medal," yelped Fat Stuff. "Right here, over my tummy."

"Shut up," muttered Kahn. "Why don't you take your stupid medal and shove it."

Fat Stuff looked at him. "You want it?" he whispered. His teeth were stained with chocolate. "I'm always open to offers, you know."

"Aw, you wouldn't sell it," said Mel. "Who are you kidding?"

"No. I mean it," said Fat Stuff, looking serious. The Blues stopped laughing.

Mel drew closer. "How much?" Everyone was staring. His own medal!

Fat Stuff gazed at the floor, thought a minute, then looked up. "A million dollars!" he grinned. "Take it or leave it."

Randy stomped out of the locker room, onto the windy, dust-filled Parade Grounds. He looked at the Omongo flag flapping wildly against the dark, mournful sky. His legs were covered with goosepimples.

"That was some lousy trick, Levine."

Randy turned. "If it hadn't been for you, Greenberg, I'd have scored."

"So that's why you tried to grab it from me," said Norman. "So you could score. You and nobody else."

"You'd have loused it up. You don't know how to swim worth beans."

Yells. At the other end of the boat house.

"A fight!"

"Counselors!"

"On the pier."

They ran.

Tannenbaum was down with Cohen and Flinn on top of him. "You lie to the old man about me," cried Flinn, "and all you'll have is a corpse."

"Let me at him," yelled Cohen. Sid tried to get up. Flinn took hold of his curly hair.

"Punch 'im in the belly," yelled Fat Stuff. "That's where it really hurts."

"Come on," cried Cohen. "You hit him enough. Tannenbaum's learned his lesson."

"I sure don't want to be in the Lieutenant's way when he gets mad."

CASUALTY

"WHAT THE HELL IS THIS!"

Norman ran up.

"It's for you, Norm. Take it," whispered Sid.

It was the cup, white, all white, perfect!

"Look, Greenberg's got himself a little clay pot to piss in."

Sid got to his feet. Flinn blocked his path. "Forget about your boy friend," he shouted. "He's got to be in the canoe race."

Norman drew the cup closer, circled by their taunting

faces. Cohen was out in front, eying the cup as if it were a weapon. Suddenly he reached out.

"Give it back!"

Cohen snatched it away. He smashed it against the pier. "There," he shouted, stamping it to pieces, "now maybe you'll break out of your little dream world." Cohen blew his whistle. "Into your canoes," he commanded. "Before it gets too dark."

The sky glistened like a velvet shroud. The wind slapped across the water, past the raft, along the pier.

A piece of white-glazed clay rolled between the slats, then sank into the foaming water below. The cup. In pieces. Even the pieces gone. Those goddam bastards!

The sky grew darker. The water was covered with pimples, white, like running sores. Norman grabbed hold of the paddle. A whistle. His paddle, raising itself above the water. *Ready, get set.* His fingers numb, as if he was on an operating table. *Go!*

The wind knifing into the water again and again like a killer gone mad. The murky sky dropping down on them. Behind it, blackness. The gray water socking against the raft, the pier, the canoes, wham, wham . . .

Cohen lifted his binoculars. "Damn! It's Greenberg! He's winning!"

"It's raining!"

"Just a few drops."

"Just the wind."

The canoes, like dying soldiers, moving from side to side, wobbling, circling.

"They're tipping over."

The wind churned the voices into a single, meaningless REDBLUREDBLU WIN WIN WIN.

Could you beat that! Little Normy Greenberg, the lousiest kid in the whole camp, paddling for all he was worth.

"Come on," shouted Cohen. "Come on, Norm baby. You're goin' to win." He stopped. So what if he was a judge? Damn it, this was his own camper, from his own tent.

"They're bailing out."

"Some race."

Steiner's voice trumpeted over the loudspeaker: "Fellow Tribesmen, the contest is over. Return to the pier."

"You'll make it," cried Cohen. "Keep going. Come on, baby. Come on, Norm."

The water was up to his ankles. Faster. Faster. His arms digging, digging, digging. A spade. A shovel. A grave. Deeper. The water. From all sides, pouring into the canoe. The cup. The cup. Sid! Don't! Don't think. Hate them. Hate them. The rocks, like statues, huge gray statues of clay, calling to him. His mother. His father. Everyone. Win. Win. Show them. His paddle going faster, faster, cutting into them, ripping them to pieces. No. They were coming in on *him*. The water, the voices, the counselors, the Reds, the Blues, pouring in, hundreds and hundreds of them, sinking him, their wind voices shrieking. He was over! In the water! His sneaker. His paddle. Win. Too late. Cold hands. Around his neck. Hundreds of cold, wet fingers. Flinn's and Cohen's and Mel's and Mike's and Steiner's and Randy's. Choking him. Pulling him down. Smashing him. Again and again. The water. The hands. The shrieks. The vase. Killim. Mama. Mama. NO NO NO NO . . .

"Win! Win baby, win baby," cried Cohen. Someone banged into his elbow. The binoculars swerved across the lake. Greenberg was lost.

"Over," sputtered the electric voice. "The race is over."

FIRST CLUE

▬▬▬▬▬▬▬▬▬▬▬▬▬▬▬▬▬

THE SKY, empty, godless, moonless, starless; Flinn's voice, dirging like a priest's; his rosary, a score card; his robe, a dirty sweatshirt; his cross, a tin medal. Father Flinn, at the edge of the pier, exhorting, waving his arms, muttering, praying. "Win, you Reds! You gotta, you gotta, you gotta!"

Gotta. His last chance. The cup or nothing. Randy felt as if the Lieutenant were talking just to him, as if everyone were staring at him, the scholarship camper who was about to win the biggest thing of all, the treasure hunt.

"Ready?" shouted the Great White Father.

"You betya," they roared.

"Judge Cohen, read the first clue."

Silence. Like a roomful of relatives trying to catch the last words of someone rich and dying. "First clue . . ." cried Cohen, as the wind howled. They looked at him, at his expression, at anything that might be a hint: the frown that went with one word; the trace of a smile when he repeated something; the slightest quiver of his lips; a weakening of his voice; a glance toward some hidden spot.

The rattling of paper magnified a thousand times, like a mirror catching the last droplets of the dying man's breath. Bodies pressing against each other.

Cohen's voice, loud and shrill:

[201]

"In a shack, there's a quack,
You all know his name.
Look under a wheel, and ye shall find
The second clue in the game."

"A wheel."

"The station wagon!"

"Quack!"

"That's Eagle all right."

The wind sang, repeating it, telling them where it was. The clouds began to spread out. The moon cast its pale light to the ground. Then it would disappear and the camp would be a nightmare of cries; of people falling, running, stumbling. They should have brought their flashlights. But it was too late.

Randy poked his head under the hood. Wheels! Wheels! Thousands of wheels! Someone yanked at the battery. The whole thing came flying out.

"It sure ain't here."

"Not a thing."

They ripped at the seats. They slashed at the spare tire.

"Inside the wheels. Of course."

They lunged into the tires with their pocket knives. The sharp hiss of escaping air.

"Ain't here."

"Not this one."

The station wagon stood on four battered stumps. Randy tore into the glove compartment. Who said anything about that? Under a wheel. *Under.*

Someone whispered it. As a joke at first. "A shack. Arts and crafts. A quack. Tannenbaum. The wheel . . ."

"You got it, Goldy, you got it!"

The yelling mob charged down the road, Seniors and Intermediates out in front, Midgets and Juniors behind like a pack of mongrel dogs.

A short cut! Randy stumbled through the woods. It was too dark. He ran back to the road. Now they were ahead of him. What if they'd already found it? "No," he cried. "No!"

He shoved his way through the door. It was like a subway, filled with hundreds of pushing, shoving, smashing campers. Tannenbaum was being held down by half a dozen husky Seniors as the others ripped into his packed suitcases.

"Where is it, Tannsy? Tell us or we'll break your goddam arm."

"The bandages. Maybe it's under . . ."

Randy stripped the adhesive from Tannenbaum's jaws. It wasn't there.

Even the Midgets were in on it, breaking the windows, shattering the pottery. The floor was sticky with clay and water and glazes, a thousand different colors, as if it were a giant palette and they, the angry artists.

A voice from the other end of the room. "Here it is!"

MIRROR MIRROR
ON THE WALL

SOMEONE GRABBED the slip and stood up on the table:

"*Behind a looking glass*
In a house that's old and new,
Seek and ye shall find
Your third clue."

"Glass?"
"What house?"

[203]

Randy ran outside. The moon had fled. Looking glass. Mirrors. House. The shit house! He could hear them yelling and screaming back there, trying to figure it out.

He crashed through the swinging doors. He fumbled for the switch. A pack of Midgets poured through after him. "Find it yourself," he shouted. Randy grabbed one, lifted him over his head, and carried him into the shower room. Cries of "Help!" He threw the kid down on the tile floor and turned on the scalding water. They stared at him like frightened animals. What was he doing? How was he going to find any clues, wasting his time like this?

The light! The others had seen! They piled through the doors. They were already at it, looking behind mirrors, yanking them from the wall, throwing them on the floor. The hot water was still on. The place was filling up with steam.

Mirror. It could be anywhere. A house. The tents. No, a house. That's what the clue said. *In a house, old and new* . . .

"Steiner's," someone blurted out.

"Colonial. That's old. And it's new, too!"

This time it was Randy who followed. There was still a chance; there were still plenty of clues; three more.

He'd find it first. He'd destroy it. The rules said you had to put it back. But he'd trick them; he'd tear the clue up into lousy little pieces.

They were ahead of him. Turning the place inside out. The bathroom. Toothpaste, shaving cream, brushes, ointments spread across the floor.

A light from under a door. Someone inside. "Here. It's here."

"Break it down."

The door flung open. "What do you . . ."

They trampled over her. In a second they were at her bureau mirror, trying to pull it down from its hooks.

"Stop it!" cried Mrs. Steiner. "The mirror's screwed on."

"Screw you."

"Get out or I'll make him call it off."

A bottle of Amour du Mal tumbled to the floor. The plate-glass mirror crashed. "The clue!"

AHEAD

"GET OUT OF HERE," cried Sylvia.

He started to read: " 'Under a . . .' "

"Out!"

A strapping Senior gripped her arm. She shivered. "O.K.," said the Senior. "Go ahead, she'll keep quiet." Everyone laughed.

"Under a plate, don't come home late,
Or for you there will be none;
Lift it up, please carefully,
And a fourth clue you shall see."

"Hell," said Fat Stuff. "It's easy. Plates. Dishes. You come home late, you don't get any. That's the . . ." They raced away to the Mess Hall.

Those dopes! Randy almost started to laugh. They were all wrong! He was running across the Parade Grounds, alone, the only one now, the only one who knew.

The ball field. He was breathing so hard he was afraid

someone would hear him. The plate. *Under a plate.* He turned it over. *Don't come home late.*

Not there! Maybe the others were right. Maybe it really was around the kitchen. He should have followed them. The moon slid behind a cloud.

The plate. Home plate. Of course! On the *Senior* field, not the Intermediate's. That was it.

He lifted the white rubber square. If only it wasn't so dark. He turned the plate over. There! Pasted on the underside, the paper, the clue, like a thousand-dollar bill.

A piece of moon winked at him. He could just make it out:

You're getting close, you're getting close,
Don't let it stump you now.
You pass it marching every day,
The fifth clue's on its way.

Where? The clue could be anywhere. *Don't let it stump you now.* But he *was* stumped. *You're getting close.* Stumped! Stump. He tore the paper into bits. The clue flew into the wind. He was way ahead of them now, and the clue, the missing link, was gone forever.

STUMPED

IIIIIIIIIIIIIIIIIIIIIIIIIIIIIIIIIIIIIIIIIIII

HE WASN'T JUST AHEAD of them, he'd already won. It was in the bag. Packed away. With his name on it. The moon was gone. He couldn't even see the rows between the tents. He ran carefully now, slower, taking no chances.

Chickens, hopping around, cackling, scratching, running in front of him, trying to block his way. He kicked at them.

He started to climb. In the branches. That's where the clue was. The chickens squawking as if their heads were going to be sliced off. As if they were going to lose, be defeated, slaughtered.

"There!"

"In the leaves!"

They were coming after him! The whole camp! Two hundred of them, pointing, yelling at him! It wasn't fair! They hadn't even found the clue!

The chickens followed, as if even they were after the cup. And now, Eagle, pointing up, shouting to the others, about it being his; the tree was his, he kept shouting. They couldn't do it. It was the last tree, the last tree.

He'd never find it. There were a million leaves, a hundred million. It would take all night. They were crawling up the trunk. He should have kicked them down.

"The clue," he shouted. "The last clue. You got to find it."

"You found it for us."

"It's not fair," he shouted.

"Nothing says we gotta find every clue."

He looked into their snarling, greedy faces. Damn them. Long as you crossed the finish line first; that's all that counted. He'd done their work for them. They were crawling up like bugs, like lice, sticking to him. If only he could pick them off, squash them, whack them, burn them.

Maybe it was somewhere else. Since when was this a stump? Those chickens croaking. Eagle shouting it was his, his. Like a nightmare.

The stump! That's it! Eagle was supposed to have

chopped the tree. They thought it'd be down when they made the clues, nothing but a stump.

He sneaked down the tree. Don't let them see him. One slip and he was finished. Think about something else. Anything else. His mother. His father. The cup. No! Don't think of it!

Inch by inch, searching, making believe it really was up there, as if the clue, the clue . . . Crackerjacks, television. Don't let them see it in his face, his eyes. Making believe he didn't already know, he worked his way down.

"Where the hell is it?"

A Senior. Randy shrugged. "Don't know," he said. As if he was one of them. Closer. The last branch. One more.

"We'll never find it here."

"How do you know it's supposed to be in the tree? It said a plate, didn't it?"

"Yeah, but we're skipping that clue."

"Where is he?"

"Who?"

"The guy who found it."

"I don't know. In the tree somewhere."

Somewhere. Closer. Closer.

"He was here a second ago. He's the one who knows, all right. Find him and you got the . . ."

"Where the hell is he?"

Almost there. Careful. Don't show it. Look like everyone else, like he didn't know. They'd see it, his face lighting up like a piece of gold. The cup, his face reflected in it. His arms around it, hugging it. Jesus. It was his. It was his.

He was on the ground. His hands embraced the tree trunk as if it were the cup, something precious, something which held the secret, the clue. He tried to look as if he were just feeling around for a penny, a lousy, worthless penny.

He felt it! Touching his fingers, at the base of the tree. Carefully, he took hold, together with the dirt and pebbles. It was in his fist now, his tight fist. Slowly he opened. He crouched low. A wrapper! A goddam candy wrapper!

Lousy trick. He fell to his knees. His fingers clawed wildly at the trunk. He couldn't help it now. There wasn't time. He had to hurry. Time was running out.

"Here it is!"

He looked up in horror, as if looking to heaven, to God, please, don't let them, don't let them.

"Hell, I was wrong. It's just a leaf."

"You ass."

Hurry. Hurry. His eyes on the ground now. At the base of the tree, the bastard tree which was hiding the secret, clinging to it, refusing to surrender.

Someone stepped on his fingers. Let them. Who cared? Long as he found it first.

"Anything there?" A stupid Junior, looking down at him.

Randy shrugged. "No," he muttered, trying to look as if he was hardly interested. "Nothing here."

Jerk! Did he think if he found it he'd make a big announcement, let everyone in on his secret, break the cup into two hundred pieces! The guy walked away.

His fingers dug frantically. Hurry. The dirt. It was loose. Someone had been there. The clue! He cupped his hand over it. He rose to his feet. He walked away, playing it dumb, looking down as if he were still searching for the clue, in his hand, all his!

He tripped over a chicken. "Get the hell outa here," he shouted, as if the chicken were his enemy, too.

The sweat poured down his face. Slowly he opened his fingers. He brought the clue to his lips. He kissed it.

Dope! They could have seen him! He buried it in his palm. He was reading a crib sheet at school, without a second to waste, with the teacher, there, looking around, two hundred teachers, trying to catch him, to expel him.

His fingers trembled. He started to read. Slowly, slowly, the prayer:

> *Blood is Red,*
> *Violets are Blue,*
> *Bring me the head of a chicken*
> *And I'll give you your next clue.*
> *Lt. Flinn.*

How could he? He didn't even have his knife. Was it a joke! A head. Ahead. That's what it meant. Ahead. He started to laugh.

He lunged. The chicken screwed up its neck, hooted, then waddled away. He had to be faster.

There. The same chicken. Looking the other way, at the campers, as they ripped the tree apart, breaking its limbs, tearing off the leaves, with Eagle screaming that it was his, they were killing his tree. Kill, that's what he had to do. How else could you win if you didn't step on someone, if you didn't push them out of your way, kick them, choke them, wring their necks with your bare hands?

He had to fight something inside him that wanted him to lose. He had to choke it, keep it down, cork it up, strangle it before it strangled him. He had to crush it, kill it, to win inside of him. The blood, the chicken, the soft, mushy guts.

It wasn't even an animal. Looking at him with its little button eyes. Straight at him. His hands, like pliers, tightening. The chicken, still looking. Like the turtle. His own. Choking it. Squeezing out its life, its blood, its insides. He was going to throw up. The neck. It was hanging by a thread now. One yank and . . .

There! On the ground, the chicken's body, jerking as if it wouldn't die, still moving, coming back at him, back to attack him. Eyeless. Mouthless. Hopping toward him.

In his palm, the rest of it, the crown, the head, red and sticky, on his wrist, dripping down his sweatshirt.

It was over. The vomit crawling along the ground. He'd won. It was out of his system.

HEADLESS

THEY'D SEEN HIM! Quick. Between the tents. Running, running down the long black windpipe. The tongue, the big wet tongue. In his hand. The head, wiggling, screaming, calling out, telling them to follow, to catch him, to stop him. He crashed into a wall. The head! Lost!

He felt in his pocket for the matches. No, they'd see! He had to. He lit one. The wind blew it out. Another. His fingers covered with blood, hot and sticky, like red glue. There, touching his sneaker. The eyes still staring. He grabbed it.

Run. The voices. Behind him. "Where?" "Clue." "Chicken." "That's him."

He had to reach Flinn. They were behind him now, all of them. With drawn knives, with daggers. And the chickens. Chasing him too. With their sharp beaks ready to peck at his flesh, to jab him, slash him. The road. Straight ahead. They were lost. They were looking for him in the tents. There, Flinn, his tall ramrod body at attention. He grabbed Flinn's hand and dropped the bloody head into the leathery palm.

Flinn reached into his pocket. "Here."

[211]

"They're chasing me. They'll be here any second."

"Go," whispered Flinn. "You're winning."

"I can't read it," cried Randy. "It's too dark."

"Stoop down. Quick so they won't see us." Flinn lit a match.

Hurry. His red fingers fastened to the paper.

The 7th clue and last clue
Is near someone named———
Race to the pier, Red or Blue,
And you my boy shall win.

"I don't get it," cried Randy.

"Don't ask me," shouted Flinn. "I'm not supposed to tell."

Howls. Cries.

"Look. A light!"

"The road."

"Let's go."

"What's it mean?" begged Randy.

"Don't you see?" whispered Flinn.

"No!" His hands trembled as they clutched the worthless clue. "I can't think straight."

"It rhymes," said Flinn.

"With what?" cried Randy. "I don't get it."

"Win. Win. Me. F' Christ's sake, it rhymes with me. Win. Flinn. It's behind the bush. You want Gans to give it away? Grab it and scram. Hurry. To the pier."

Randy reached in. A trick! The bush was all covered with thorns. No. Something big. Metal. He picked it up.

"There he is!"

"I see 'em all right."

"Let's get 'em."

HOLOCAUST

THE CUP! The cup! In his own two bleeding hands. It was his. He started to run. No. They were blocking the way. Coming toward him. The cup was big, heavy. If only he had a minute to rest, to catch his breath, to wipe the sweat away, to wipe the blood away. The tents. Where they couldn't see him. Hurry!

It was dark. He fell. The cup was still in his arms. He felt dead.

The cup! How could he let someone else get it! When his own hands were already holding it, when his own brain had already doped it out, had already tricked them, was already winning, winning.

They were behind now, way behind, talking to Flinn. Flinn would stall them, get them off his track. If only he could last. A wall, like a boxing glove. The cup was on the ground. He crawled toward it. Get up. Where was it? The matches. Only three left now. There! He hugged it to his breast. He kissed it. "I'm going to win you!" he cried. "I'm going to win!" The match died out.

The road. No. They'd catch him. He picked up a branch. Another match. "Don't go out. Don't go out," as he huddled over it like a beggar, a rich beggar, the big gold cup in his hand. It was on fire. He had a torch now. He held it up high.

Torch in one hand, cup in the other, he ran. Faster. They'd see him. He held the cup closer. It was his, his.

Behind him. He could hear them, crashing into walls, breaking their legs, arms, their backs. Good!

"The light."

"That's him."

"Get him!"

Run. Run. The whole camp was after him, chasing, trying to catch him, beat him, kill him. He stopped. Trick them. He raised the torch. Tent 38. He lit it. The flames, roaring into the sky. The cup was his. It had to be.

"No!"

"Look, he's . . ."

"No! No!" cried Steiner. "The camp's on fire."

"Too late," screamed Sylvia. "Too late, White Father."

"Help. Omongo."

Indians! Eagle shook his fists. His own people. The Omongos. The camp. Steiner's camp. Burning. Steiner, with a little bucket of water, trying to put out the flames. Another tent. Another. Eagle let out his war cry. Another. Another. The whole camp, burning. His people. His.

It was his. The cup. They'd never get him. He'd tricked them. Past the Parade Grounds. Back of him. The voices. Shouting. The camp. Like a Bible city consumed in flames. They were stopping. He was free, free to win. Like a pirate, his trunk filled with gold, sailing down the bay, not in a canoe, but a ship with sails, with flags, with cannons roaring. The cup. In the crow's nest. He was holding it up for everyone on the shore to see. Cheering as the cup sailed by. Past the Boat House. His torch. The heat closing in on his fingers. The finish line. In white chalk. Marked out at the end of the pier. He looked at the water, black and angry. A sneaker. Twigs. A broken paddle. Back and forth in the water as if a ghostly hand were still moving it. As if it were still trying to win. He threw the torch into the lake. With a hiss, it struck the dead paddle, then sank into the diseased water.

"Get him!"

"Stop him!"

"I'll kill him, kill him!"

"Levine!"

"It's Levine!"

Behind him. Yelling at him, cursing him, jealous, closing in. He started down the pier, toward the line, his arms and legs dangling, as if he were a puppet, as if he were dying, coming apart, the fake tears pouring down his face, his wooden mouth gasping, as the cries grew closer, closer, as he took hold with his trembling arms, and with all his strength triumphantly hoisted the toy cup above him as he leaped over the finish line, shouting, as if in a dream, a nightmare from which he would never awake: "I won! I won!"

ABOUT THE AUTHOR

BURT BLECHMAN created a literary sensation with the publication of his first novel, *How Much?*, in 1961. Critical acclaim came from W. H. Auden, Saul Bellow, Alfred Kazin, columnists and commentators, and culminated in Lillian Hellman's dramatization of the satire for Broadway under the title *My Mother, My Father and Me*.

When not working on books and plays, Mr. Blechman spends his time traveling. A native New Yorker, he has also lived in Mexico City and Rio de Janeiro, has made eight trips to Europe, and has visited most of the countries of Latin America. He was in Cuba during the revolution.

At sixteen, the author left home to join the Merchant Marine. Later he financed his career by working as a farmhand, realtor, waiter, census taker, *New York Times* adtaker, and shoe corporation executive.

Burt Blechman used to be sent away to summer camp every year.